BAUBLES FROM BONES

> Fall 2024 <

Shane Gallaher ·· *Editor*
Elyse Leskovic ·· *Editor, Artist*
Joel Troutman ··································· *Editor, Typesetter*
Caroline Ritzert ························· *Social Media Manager*

Cover art: shugarkyub

Illustrations: Elyse Leskovic: *(25, 48, 50, 53, 74, 75, 97, 106, 107, 115, 117, 131)*, Joel Troutman: *(27, 81, 95, 109, 134, 136, 137)*

Baubles From Bones: Issue 2, Fall 2024 ISBN 979-8-218-49193-2. Independently published and distributed: Pittsburgh, PA. Printed in USA. Copyright © 2024, Baubles From Bones. All rights reserved.

baublesfrombones.com

TABLE OF CONTENTS

⸜ FICTION ⸝

⸜ POETRY ⸝

⸜ EDITORIAL ⸝

THE PUZZLE VAULT

Auston Habershaw

Only fools or relatives came to Posto Nessum, and the four men on horseback were no relatives of Beatriz Faro's. She paused in sweeping the dust off the steps of her shop and squinted against the heat of the rising sun. Four men on hardy Eddon steppe horses, with a fifth horse in tow. The men were armed, too.

Yes, definitely fools.

"Benito!" she yelled to the boy drawing water from the well. He, too, was watching the horsemen approach. Ten years old, now—he had the look of his late father. Gangly, with golden eyes fixed far away. Sometimes it made her heart skip to look at him.

"I've almost got the water, Mamma!"

"Hush! Go inside. Lock the door."

Benito frowned and looked at the men. "But, Mamma—they will be thirsty!"

"They can draw their own water—go now!" The boy caught her eye and went. When Beatriz heard the bolt slam home behind her, she breathed easier. Hann bless him, but he was a good boy. Fools were better dealt with when there were no children about.

A few minutes later, the men rode through the gap in the ancient stone walls of the old outpost and around the well in the courtyard. They peered into the open doorways of the abandoned buildings on either side before deigning to greet her.

"There is nobody living in those places," she said to them. "The barracks have been abandoned for ten years, the stable has no horses in it, the guardhouse is full of dust and sand weasels. If you're looking for someone to talk to, señors, I am it."

One of the men dismounted. His boots were of good quality, but well-worn. His cape was dusty and tattered, but had once been a fine garment—the clothing of an almost or once-rich man. He bowed in a manner more fitting to a court. "I am Carlos Santuva de Otove y Norada. My companions and I are looking for a guide."

"I am the guide." Beatriz said. "There are very few places to go from here, señor."

Santuva smiled. His men smiled, too. "I believe you know where we want to go."

Beatriz grimaced. *Fools.* "The Puzzle Vault."

"Your fee." Santuva produced a small bag and threw it to her. It jingled, but not enough.

"The fee is *per man*, señor."

Santuva laughed. The men laughed, too. "That is very expensive for you just to show us a door."

Beatriz planted her feet. "It is not just for that." *It's for dragging your bodies out of the dark. It's for defending myself from your anger when you fail. It's for making me return to that cursed room and making me relive its horrors. It's for a thousand reasons.*

Santuva shook his head. "Very well." He jerked his head towards his men, who dismounted and began to tend to their horses. One produced a somewhat larger bag and gave it to Santuva, who in turn gave it to Beatriz. "How long will the journey take?"

Beatriz checked the sun. "If we leave now, we will arrive at nightfall, but your men need to water their horses and I must get ready, so we should expect to camp before reaching the entrance to the vault. You may attempt it in the morning."

Santuva smiled. "Excellent. Perhaps some refreshment, then?"

"This is not a café. The well is behind you. Excuse me."

Benito let her in. She locked the door behind her. "Benito," she said, "go and get my things."

———————◆•◆———————

Beatriz gave Benito the keys to the strongbox, told him how to go for help if she did not return, and made him recite the names and homesteads of their closest five relatives. She took time in the small family shrine to say her prayers to Hann—one for Benito, for protection; one for her daughter Inez, for guidance with her new husband far away; and two for her husband Juan and her eldest son Alonso, for forgiveness. Then she took her satchel full of illumite shards, sparkstones, and enchanted rope, threw her talismans around her neck, and went out to meet Santuva's band. Benito locked the door behind her. *Good boy.*

The men were already mounted. Santuva put his hand out to help her up into the saddle. "Are you ready, señora? The sun is almost at its peak."

Beatriz ignored his hand and brought the mule out of the stable. "You will be trying the Vault tomorrow, one way or another." She mounted the beast and tapped her heels against his side. "Follow me."

Outside the crumbling walls of Posto Nessum, Beatriz wrapped her face in a headscarf and thanked Hann for the dust talisman she wore that kept the terrible grit of sand from her eyes. It was hot and Santuva's horses were tired, so they kept a modest pace as they rode across the dry steppes, their capes fluttering in the harsh winds that came off the wastes.

Santuva rode abreast of her. "Once you take us to the entrance to the vault, what is to stop us from telling anyone we please where it may be found?" He took a swig from his canteen. "Perhaps I could start a competing guide service, eh? Make my money back."

"True, but then you would have to live out here." She gestured to the pan-flat brown of the steppes, stretching off as far as could be seen, with nothing but the swirl of dust devils for scenery.

Santuva grunted, conceding the point. "And why do *you* live out here, señora?"

Beatriz did not let herself scowl. "If I did not, who would lead fools to the Puzzle Vault, señor?"

Santuva laughed. This time, his men did not.

The men were mercenaries, clearly. Two Verisi and an Illini, the former wearing colorful, patterned headscarves and neatly trimmed goatees and the latter wearing a black cap and a long black moustache. All three wore swords and had bows lashed to their saddles. When they spoke, they spoke Verisi among themselves. Beatriz could understand some of it—the language was not so different from her native Rhondian—but missed some of the more complex lewd jokes. All she knew was that the jokes were about her. Her skin crawled. *Why do I do this? Why do I keep going back?*

The answer was there, though. It had always been there. Only Beatriz refused to face it, to admit to it. As always.

There was little shelter to be had among the sagebrush and tree-like cacti of the steppe, so when the sun began to kiss the western horizon, she suggested they set camp beside a great orange boulder where a thick concentration of brush grew. Santuva agreed.

"Should we light a fire?" The Illini—a man named Ozzik—asked.

"Do you like being cold?" Beatriz said.

"No bandits?"

Beatriz laughed as she hauled the saddle off her mule. "Who would they rob? Me? You? We are too far from any caravan route to worry. Build a fire. I am not so young that I enjoy the evening chill."

And so the fire was built, and one of the Verisi took out a bone flute to play. The music—some sea shanty—was bright and lively. The small party shared its food with Beatriz, and with them she shared some of her own provisions—dried fruit and nuts, a small wedge of hard cheese. Besides Beatriz, the mood among them was light.

Ozzik the Illini was passing a flask of ouzo around. Beatriz took a sip and was pleased to find that the flask had an enchantment on it that kept the liquor very cold, just as it would have been served in an Illini café. It made her shiver. "You are a well-equipped party." Beatriz said, holding the flask up to the Illini in salute.

Santuva reclined against the boulder. "I am a man of means. I pay my followers well." He leaned forward. "And yet you do not seem to like us very much. I saw how you hid your son from us, how you barred your door against us." He put his hand out for the flask. "Not very hospitable, señora."

"I have my reasons." Beatriz handed him the flask. "I do not commonly encounter gentlemen in the wastes."

Santuva laughed. "There is an exception to every rule, señora—and here I am!"

Beatriz permitted herself a tight smile. "We shall see."

"What can we expect tomorrow? I have heard so much and yet so little about the Vault. What can you tell me?"

The flute fell silent. Beatriz looked across the fire at the other men. They were all listening now. "It is hard to explain. I can tell you that most of you will probably die, and those of you that live will blame me for what happens to the others."

"Why? What is so fiendish that guards the treasure?" Santuva gestured towards his saddlebags. "I have antispell, wards, talismans, weapons—what could it be?"

Beatriz closed her eyes. She could picture the Vault clearly, as though it were etched in her eyelids. "The warlock king who devised the Puzzle Vault knew his enemies would seek to plunder his treasures with sorcery and brute force, so he devised a trap that uses no sorcery and cannot be overcome by force of arms. Within is a lion's head. One of you must put your arm inside the lion's mouth. This will open the shaft leading down to the maze and, beyond that, the treasure vault itself, but the man who puts his arm in will be trapped. Those of you who descend will have exactly three minutes to solve the maze, enter the vault, pillage what you can, and return."

"And the man who puts his arm in? What happens to him?" The Illini asked.

Beatriz opened her eyes. "He dies."

The men looked dumbstruck. Santuva scowled. "What kind of a puzzle is that? Nobody mentioned this! Of all the men I spoke to who had come here, not one had—"

"Tell me, señor, if *you* had forced one of your companions to sacrifice his life for your own enrichment, would you share the tale with others?" Beatriz shook her head. "No doubt they all warned you against coming, assuming they had any decency in them."

Santuva stroked his goatee. "There must be some trick, some catch."

Beatriz hugged her knees to her chest. "The fact that you have come this far and invested this much to claim the treasure means you will fail, by definition. If you are wise, you will realize this before it is too late." Beatriz looked deep into the fire, blinding herself with the light. "Most men are not so wise as that."

"And yet men have brought wondrous treasures from the depths of the vault." Santuva countered. "I know this. I have seen them with my own eyes in the palaces of Itiara and Veris and Ihyn."

Ah, he is from a merchant family, then? Beatriz rubbed her hands to hide how they shivered. "Bought with the blood of their friends, and spread out over two thousand years. For every bauble that escapes the clutches of that fiendish Vault, a hundred expeditions end in failure."

Santuva stroked his goatee for a moment, contemplating the stars. "In all things, señora, I strive to be the exception."

Beatriz had heard words like this before—from the lips of her husband, Juan. She could still see those faraway eyes, looking up at the night sky just as Santuva did now, and hear his cool voice speaking of the same treasures and the ambition that would see them realized. The memory hurt like a cut. As always, she pushed it away. She focused on the fire, on the cold air, on the ordeal to come.

No one said anything more— Beatriz had spoiled the mood. She pulled her blanket roll up to her chin and lay down to sleep. As the fire died, she could hear the singing of desert toads and the chirps of the crickets they fed on. She shivered. And slept.

———————◆◆◆———————

They made the Vault by midmorning the next day. Beatriz could always tell when they were getting close—the air was no longer as dry, and her black hair began to frizz up into clumps beneath her scarf. The plants on the ground grew greener. Birdsong could be heard. It was around then that they found the river.

The Guasto River was not much of a river, at least not by this point. It began up in the Artavi Mountains away in the west and ran to its death in the wastes, splintering into little streams and creeks, never to find the sea. This particular stream was one of the larger remnants— about twenty feet wide and three or four feet deep at its deepest point. It ran swiftly, though, and the silt bottom shifted easily underfoot—

Beatriz told them it was unwise to cross on horseback. They paused to water the horses.

"We will be there soon." Beatriz said in answer to Santuva's questioning look. "We follow the river east a bit further, and then we will see it."

The river terminated in a crack in the earth itself—a ragged maw of stone that swallowed the water entirely in its dark, crashing depths. Here a hitching post had been driven into the ground by ancient hands, long since dead. Beatriz dismounted and tied up her mule. The others did the same. "Bring your things," she said, "the entrance is down there." She pointed into the chasm. "Once we are on the stair, the sound of the water will be too loud for us speak over. If you have any questions before you enter the Vault, ask them now."

"Will we need weapons?" The Illini asked.

"Probably not." Beatriz checked her talismans— all present.

The Illini raised an eyebrow. "Probably?"

"Only if you intend to use them on each other."

At this, the men left their bows. All of them wore their swords; even Santuva strapped on a gentleman's rapier.

The stairs down to the Vault were impossible to see unless you knew where to look. A narrow set of water-worn stone steps, they were cut into the side of the cavern ages ago and became so slick and uneven that previous expeditions had to set iron rings into the wall and run a rope to aid in the descent. When these iron rings had rusted away and the ropes rotted to nothing, new ones had been added. And then others. And others after that. The last set— the set Beatriz and her husband had installed— were of mageglass, and so would never rot nor rust nor spoil. She spoke a word, and her enchanted rope flew from her satchel and threaded itself through each ring. She put a shard of illumite around her neck on a leather string and set off down the precarious steps, one hand clutching the rope.

The sound of the river crashing into the darkness below was an overwhelming, bludgeoning force. The mist stung her dry cheeks. She kept her eyes fixed on the steps and a firm grip on the rope. On her last trip here— about five months ago— a new stair had given way, and one of the treasure hunting party had fallen into the abyss.

They descended until the light from above was thin and pale, filtered through the water vapor thrown off by the falls. The stairs stopped at a small landing, ten feet across. An ancient stone sconce was set into the wall beside a broad door. Beatriz fished another piece of illumite from her satchel and placed it there, illuminating the floor beneath their feet. It was not a natural landing— square flagstones, smooth and gray.

Beyond the door was another stairway, this one better preserved and not at the edge of an abyss. It was wide and descended beneath vaulted ceilings. Beatriz had heard that the walls had once been gilded with gold and embedded with jewels and mosaics of jade, but thieves over the ages had stripped them bare.

Eventually the roar of the falls dimmed behind them so that Beatriz could hear their footfalls. Santuva whistled. "It will be some feat, raising treasure from this depth." He looked back at his men. "You boys will be earning your pay for certain." They all laughed.

"No one has ever had that problem before." Beatriz said. She thought of all the bodies, broken and bloody, that she had dragged up these stairs over the years or cast into the abyss. Her hands shook. She was about to do it again. *Forty pieces of silver is not enough. It is never enough. And yet I come, again and again.*

At last the stairs stopped and they stood before a grand archway. On either side stood stone colossi, their features marred beyond all recognition by the greedy picks and axes of thieves. Bones, broken and yellow with age, piled in the corners; toothless skulls leered out from rusty helms—the legacy of ancient disputes over shares of the take. Beatriz didn't pay them any heed. "Welcome to the Puzzle Vault of Askar, Fifteenth King of the dead kingdom of Shendrazail."

She looked at the men, who also wore illumite shards around their necks. Their eyes glittered in the blue-white light. Santuva's teeth seemed to glow as he smiled. "Will you come in with us?"

"I would prefer to wait here."

One of the Verisi pulled a dagger. Santuva frowned at him, but did not object. "I'm afraid we must insist. We can't have you taking your rope and abandoning us. You understand, of course."

Beatriz nodded, outwardly calm. "Of course."

Beyond the great arch was an even greater room, its vaulted dome lost in the shadows. Placed around the tiled stone floor were braziers filled with pitch-soaked straw or dried brush or whatever else would burn with a healthy flame. Beatriz left the men to explore and set about lighting them with a sparkstone until, at length, the whole chamber could be seen in the orange light of the flickering fires.

Like most other places in the Vault, the walls were picked clean up to about fifteen feet off the floor. Above this, elaborate mosaics of semi-precious stones, soot stained from ages of torchsmoke, stretched up into the shadows. They depicted horses and soldiers, demons and angels waging battle, and the fearsome visage of the Warlock King Askar XV, resplendent in gilded robes, his visage not that of a man, but that of a golden-maned lion.

"Hann's boots..." Santuva breathed, holding a torch aloft, eyes wide.

Beatriz turned. Santuva and his men stared, awestruck, at the very mechanism that would make them either rich or dead. A statue, thirty feet tall, in the form of a man with a lion's head, muscular chest burnished in gold, teeth of ivory, eyes of gleaming yellow tourmaline. The figure seemed to gaze down at them, frozen in a fearsome pose of rage and warning. One great arm was raised, holding a huge onyx khopesh. The other arm was missing—a victim of particularly ambitious raiders from some unknown time past. Its crumbled remains still lay strewn across the broad floor, the thin layer of gold long since peeled away.

"Where is the trap you spoke of?" Santuva asked.

"There." Beatriz pointed between the giant's legs. There was another lion's head, or what had once been one, before it had been bludgeoned, chipped, and cracked over the years. Its mouth was open, though, and jaws of unblemished steel were clearly visible. Down the front of this statue were black stains. At its foot was a fine layer of sand from which poked the occasional ancient bone.

The men gazed upon it in silence, each contemplating the meaning of those black stains, those ancient bones.

The Verisi with the dagger pointed it at Beatriz. "We could just make *her* do it."

Beatriz had steeled herself against this moment—there was always *this* moment. She caught up her talismans and shook them at the Verisi. "I am warded against blades and bear talismans of protection. If I do not return, my son will find my relatives, and my family will hunt you to the ends of the earth."

The Illini laughed. "Empty words, woman. The talismans probably don't even work and that boy is not going anywhere." He advanced on her.

"Wait!" Santuva stepped between them. "Ozzik, leave her be!"

The second Verisi drew his sword. Ozzik put a hand on the hilt of his saber. Beatriz backed towards the wall—towards a little alcove she had used before to escape such behavior.

"Enough! Put up your swords, men!" Santuva slashed the air with one hand. "We haven't come all this way to slay each other like pirates!" He looked at Beatriz. "Surely you must know more! There *must* be some trick!"

Beatriz shook her head. "If I told you, I would doom you all to death. Leave now! Spare all your lives!"

All four men paused. The Verisi with his sword drawn cocked his head. "Tell us anyway, signora."

Beatriz balled her hands into fists. "You must believe me!"

Ozzik sought to come closer to her, Santuva's hand on his shoulder. "You will either tell us, woman, or you will die. Your choice."

Beatriz looked at Santuva. He sighed and shrugged. "I am but one man, señora, and these men have come a *long way*. What can it hurt to tell us, eh?"

She wanted to cry, but held it in. *Hann forgive me!* She spoke quietly, each word pained. "There is a legend— *only* a legend, mind you— that there is a secret catch in the vault that would release the prisoner of the lion's head. Once struck, however, the vault will begin to close and those inside will have only a brief time to escape with their lives."

"What happens when the vault closes?" Santuva asked.

"The maze between this room and the treasure chamber fills with water from the river. Those in the vault suffocate, those in the maze drown. No one who has sought the catch has found it. Ever."

Santuva clapped his hands. "There— see! I knew there was some trick to it."

Beatriz shook her head. "Listen to me! *No one has found it!* You have only three minutes to save the life of the man in the lion's mouth— first you must negotiate the maze, then you must seize some treasure, then you must find the catch, then you must negotiate the maze on the way out. It *cannot* be done!"

Santuva smiled. "Ah, but señora, you forget that I am *exceptional.*" He reached into his shirt and drew out a scrap of thin, dried leather. On it had been inked a rectangular shape—a map.

The map.

"A map to the maze!" Ozzik shouted and stood beside Santuva to look over his shoulder. The two Verisi came up, too, after sheathing their own weapons.

Santuva let them pore over it and held his hand out to Beatriz. "There, you see? I am certain with the map to lead us through the maze, we will have plenty of time to seek the catch, yes?"

"If it exists." Beatriz came closer, but did not take his hand. She stared, instead, at the map clutched in the greedy fingers of the mercenaries. Her heart began to pound. She had seen this map before. *Gods, why do you torture us so? Why lay such traps for our failings?*

Santuva's eyes sparkled. "Just think, señora—all these years of watching men fail to best the vault, now to be on the cusp of observing their victory! You should be delighted!" He turned to his men. "Now, who shall risk the lion's maw first, eh?"

Beatriz kept her distance as they argued. She tried to calm herself, to steady her breathing, but it would not happen. The map had pushed her over the edge, and she felt like she was falling. It was all she could do to hold back tears.

Finally, the men drew lots. One of the Verisi lost, and so he rolled up his sleeve, said a prayer to Hann, and put his arm into the lion's mouth. Nothing happened. They all looked at her, expectantly. Beatriz took a deep breath. "There are five catches at the back. Hit them with each of your fingers."

He did. The lion's steel jaws clamped closed around the Verisi's upper arm. The entire chamber rumbled as a spiral stair sank into the earth at the exact center of the floor. Above them, the great arm with the great khopesh began to drop, slowly, inexorably, in an arc that would pass its ancient blade through the shoulder of the Verisi. The man looked up and began to scream. "Go! Go, my friends! Quickly!"

Santuva, Ozzik, and the other Verisi darted down the stairs, Santuva holding the map in one hand, a torch in the other. For a time, Beatriz could hear their shouts echoing from below. Then, by the time the arm was a third of the way through its arc, there was only the heavy, grinding noise of the stone arm pivoting downward.

The Verisi struggled against the trap, trying to pull his arm free. He chipped at the stone with his knife in his free hand. He growled curses. The huge blade was halfway down now. "Signora!" he called, "Help me!"

Beatriz stomach boiled. She turned her back on him as tears began to blind her eyes. It was always like this. Always. She wanted to run away. Every time they screamed, she heard her husband's voice, screaming the same way. *Help me, Beatriz! Alonso isn't finding the catch! Help me get out!*

The arm was two-thirds down now. She listened at the top of the stairs— no sound. They were not even in the maze, and only one minute remained. The trapped Verisi was beginning to panic. He clawed at his own shoulder. "For Hann's sake, help me! They are not coming back! You can help me!" She looked at him. He was holding out his knife, his eyes wide. "Cut at my arm! Cut my flesh away, signora! I...I cannot do it myself!"

Thirty seconds now. The sound of voices shouting came from below. They had not found the catch.

"Signora! *Please!*" Tears streamed down the Verisi's face. The great khopesh had almost completed its one-hundred and eighty degree arc. The man in its path looked tiny—a daisy before the scythe.

If I am merciful, I will just kill him now. She took a step towards him, but stopped.

The Verisi began to stab and slash at his own arm, trying to slice himself free from the trap. His arm slid out a bit—only to his elbow, though. He wailed in despair, blood pouring from his wounds.

Five seconds, perhaps less. Ozzik, face pale, stumbled up from the depths. His saber was drawn, but unblooded. Next came Santuva, with barely a second to spare, something clutched to his chest.

"NOOOO! NOOOOOO!" The Verisi shrieked one last time before the heavy weight of the stone khopesh tore through his arm and shoulder without the slightest pause. Blood spurted across the feet of the giant and the mane of the lion's head. The Verisi stumbled back, one-armed, looked up at the sky, and fell backwards with a gurgle. His life's blood spilled in the dust from his jagged wounds as the chamber rumbled, the khopesh returned to its original position, and the stairway sealed.

Silence.

Ozzik was on all fours, kissing the ground. Santuva sat with his back against the wall, panting. He did not look at her, nor at the dead man bleeding out on the ground. "We...we couldn't find it. Damn, that place is enormous. I...I had no idea...no idea. Nobody *told* me!"

I told you. But Beatriz said nothing.

"That fool!" Ozzik had gotten up. He looked shaken. "That fool, Antosi! He wouldn't come. He was still looking for the catch when we left him."

"Then he's still there." Beatriz said, her voice numb. "There will probably be air enough in the vault to keep him alive for a short time."

The color drained from the Illini's face. "That is a cruel thing to say."

Santuva stood up. "Perhaps he's found it! We can go back for him! Ozzik!" He jerked his head towards the lion's mouth, where the severed stump of the Verisi's arm still protruded.

"What, and trade my life for his? You're mad!" The Illini looked as though he would vomit. "I am never doing *that* again."

"But Ozzik, look at *this!*" Santuva held something to the light. It was a circlet of gold, too small for an adult—for a child, then. Emeralds studded its circumference and the shape of an eagle rising into the air was shaped into the front. Between its wings was cradled a white diamond the size of a man's thumbnail.

Ozzik looked at it for a long, quiet moment. "We cut our losses. I take the Verisi's shares—more than I bargained for anyway. We leave this place."

The Illini turned to leave, but Santuva blocked his path, took him by the shoulders. "My friend! Think of what Antosi is doing right now! He's finding the catch. He's collecting more treasure—gods, man, he probably has a sack full of crowns and jewels right now! You saw the piles, didn't you?"

The Illini pushed him away. "I saw the *bones*, Santuva. That's all I saw—that and the claw marks on the walls. The woman was right."

Beatriz went to the body of the dead man and used her own cloak to cover him up. His eyes were still open. The man had never been kind to her, that was true, but he hadn't been monstrous, either. If no one else would mourn for him, she felt at least she ought to. It was her role in this place, perhaps— to come and mourn, over and over.

Yes, there was some truth to that. She bowed her head.

"What are you doing?" The Illini pointed at the body. "Leave that alone."

"This was a man who died so you could get that crown the two of you are haggling over!" Beatriz snapped. "Have some respect for the dead."

Santuva was still pressing his case. "Ozzik, this crown is worth a tidy sum, but it's not much more than *investment* capital. It will buy you a tract of land, maybe. Perhaps a small ship with no crew to man it. Did we come all this way— did I *hire* you to come all this way and *fail* right at this moment?" Santuva put the circlet in Ozzik's hands. "The moment of truth, señor. Stick with me and become a legend or leave and die a shepherd!"

Beatriz shook her head. "Don't listen to him, Ozzik. Go. I don't feel like tending to another body, least of all yours."

The Illini handed the circlet back to Santuva. "I stay, but we put the woman's arm in the lion's mouth."

"I won't do it." Beatriz's voice cracked. "Never!"

Santuva pulled at his goatee. "You must know, señora, that I cannot walk away." He shrugged. "I need more than this to save my family from destitution. I have tried every other means I know how. I am here; I must try."

Beatriz backed towards her alcove. Ozzik moved off to her right. The two men were closing on her. "Not so exceptional after all, then," she snarled. "You can't force me. I will *never* do it."

Santuva's face darkened. The smiles and the constructed image of affluence fell away from him. His expression became as tattered as his clothing. "Ozzik: go back to the señora's house. Find her son and hold him hostage. If you do not see me in two days, kill him."

Beatriz gasped. "You miserable—"

"Ha!" Ozzik grinned, showing the gaps in his teeth. "What about my share?"

"You'll get it when I see you again. Go!" Santuva snarled. The Illini left with a snicker for Beatriz.

Beatriz glared at the Rhondian merchant. "As I said— there are no gentlemen in the wastes."

There was a moment when Santuva looked ill— he paled, gulped air, but something entered his mind and his expression darkened. "It is only three minutes, señora. Do it now— put your arm into the lion's mouth— and I will catch up to Ozzik long before he finds your boy. This does not need to happen."

Beatriz shivered with anger. She struggled to speak. "No."

Santuva drew his rapier. "I do not wish to hurt you, señora. But I must go back. I must get more than this trinket," he waved the circlet around, "I have *no choice*."

"I will never put my arm in the lion's mouth! Never, you understand?" She closed her eyes. She should not have: the image of her husband, shrieking on the ground, blood pouring from his severed arm. The sound of the vault sealing even as her eldest son was calling her name from the depths of the maze. The weight of the memory caused her to crumple. She leaned against a pile of debris and rocked, eyes closed, tears falling. "Never. Never never."

Santuva looked bewildered. "Well... then we are at an impasse, yes? I cannot leave, you cannot go forward, and so Ozzik will go and murder your son, and there will be nothing we can do about it."

Beatriz opened one eye enough to glare at him. "But for your greed, you might have left already! You might never have *come*! I might never have come to this place— not even once. I would be living in a little village outside of Via Durano with my husband and my children and we would be *poor* but we would *never* have come here! None of this would have been, but for the childish greed of men!"

"Is it childish to wish a legacy for *my* son, señora? Is it *childish* to wish that they not see their father lose all that they have known? To be reduced to living in a hovel and eating gruel and begging in the streets? Is that the wish of a *child*? Eh?" Santuva kicked a skull across the floor and threw his rapier on the ground. "All this— *all this* I do for my family! Surely you understand that! I have traveled a thousand miles to a wasteland! I have shared meals with black-hearted mercenaries like

Ozzik! I have threatened women and children! All for my *own* children! *What choice do I have?"*

Beatriz drew a shuddering breath. "You could live in a hovel and eat gruel and beg in the streets. But you would live."

Santuva put his hands to his head and pulled at his hair. "Death first. Death *first!* I will not fail them, not while I live!"

Beatriz hugged her knees to her chest. "Then we are at an impasse. As you say."

Santuva sat on the floor, head in his hands. Neither of them spoke— they each wrestled with their own demons in private for a time. Beatriz thought of all the months of preparation her husband had devoted to this room and the vault beyond. He had been an intelligent man— an *educated* man, brought up in the church, an expert in ancient languages and history. With the birth of their third child and a season of drought, he had bent all his skill and intelligence against cracking the secrets of the Puzzle Vault. They had moved here, to the abandoned outpost. He had been meticulous, cautious, rational. None of it had mattered.

That was the puzzle, Beatriz felt. She had not known it until afterwards— after both her Juan and her Alonso had died here. It did not matter what brought someone to this terrible room, be it pride, greed, curiosity, or otherwise— the fact that they were here was enough to kill them.

Santuva stood up, wiped his eyes, straightened his doublet. "My family lives in Otove. You could find them señora, yes?"

"Yes, I suppose. Why?"

Santuva strode past her, tore the bloody ruin of the Verisi's arm from the lion's mouth, and thrust his arm inside. The chamber shuddered as the mechanism came to life. "Go." He said to her, forcing a smile. "Retrieve what you can. Bring it to my family. Tell them what you like."

Beatriz stood up. Her whole body was shaking, she realized. "Why...why did you—"

"GO!"

And so she found herself going— down those horrid, ancient spiral stairs and into the darkness of the maze. It was dank and dripping with water, the slick black stone of its walls glittering in the pale light of her illumite shard. She knew the way through— her husband had the map, too, and he and Alonso used to quiz each other around the dinner table. Inez, her daughter, would get into it, as well. They had family contests— who could solve the maze fastest. All of it came rushing back to her, so vivid that it was almost as though she were there, sitting at her dinner table with her husband and eldest child alive and well, laughing as they maneuvered an olive across an oilskin reproduction of the maze.

She leapt over the bones of former adventurers, ignored the stench of rot from the more recent ones, and hurried her way down the narrow tunnels. *Straight, second left, first right, third right, first left, first right, first left and...*

She came out of the maze and into the treasure vault itself. A place she had never been and never wanted to be. It looked to be a mostly natural cave— stalactites and stalagmites of a kind of stone that sparkled in the pale light. And there— and there and there— piled in the shadows of the chamber, on ancient stone tables and in the rotted away frames of ancient chests, were treasures *undreamed* of. For all her terror and urgency, Beatriz was compelled to tarry for a moment and gaze at the wondrous things. Piles of rubies as big as grapes; statuettes of jade and alabaster and onyx, gilded in silver and adamant; crowns, necklaces, shirts of mail, torques all of gold; coins enough to swim in. Beatriz had once wondered how long it would take before the entire vault were cleaned out. Now she knew it would be another thousand years, and perhaps another beyond that before it would come to pass; an ocean of blood would have to be spilled along the way.

Something gleamed in the distant dark— the shard of illumite around Antosi's neck! Gods— how much time had she wasted gawking? She didn't know! Fire burned through her legs as she scrambled over hills of gold and pyramids of diamonds to get to the fallen Verisi.

Antosi was splayed across the armrests of a golden throne, lions rampant on its backrest, his own dagger plunged into his own heart. Dead of despair. *How much time?*

Antosi had in his hand a sack— it was heavy, and it jingled. She caught it up and threw it over her back. She turned to leave.

She stopped. Out of the corner of her eye, something *green*. Her heart pounding, she looked— there, beyond the throne, far in the back of the cavern, was a great mountain of copper coins and greaves and helms all turned bright green with a thick layer of patina. Whereas everywhere else was something that glittered with the untarnished glory of gold and gemstones, here looked like an ancient, corroded dungheap— the leavings of some lesser treasure horde, cast aside over the ages.

Of course. The catch would have to be hidden there. What burglar, pressed for time, would ever even notice it?

But how much time? If she ran, she could perhaps make it out. Or perhaps not. She had no idea! Every second she tarried put her life and the life of Benito in danger. She just had to run, and now!

And then watch as another man died horribly.

Beatriz, you are a fool, she told herself, but dove into the pile of copper armor and coins like a tiger pouncing. She threw them aside, slapping at every exposed stone, every knobby outcropping.

Something *moved*. A slate set into the floor. She pushed it and pushed it, but it would not catch. *How much time! Run girl!*

But Beatriz did not run. She instead put down the sack and grabbed the Verisi's body and dragged it over to the plate. With her and him together, the weight was enough for something to catch with a dull *clunk.*

Then she ran. Fast as her legs could carry her, slipping and skidding across the slick floors of the maze, knocking bones and rusty bits of mail aside as she went. She reached the stairs as they were beginning to rise again and wriggled through the opening at the last moment, screaming as she did so. Then there was a strong hand around her own, pulling her. She looked up.

It was Santuva, smiling at her.

It was then that she remembered: she had forgotten the sack of treasure.

They sat, side by side, backs to the wall. The fires in the braziers guttered low. Beatriz's heart seemed unable to slow. The world seemed to spin.

Santuva stroked his goatee and stared up at the sparkle of the high-up mosaics. "You didn't bring anything back."

Beatriz shook her head. "No. I'm sorry. We... I could go back. I know how."

"No. I would not do that to you," he said. He was quiet for a moment, as though seeking the proper words. "I must beg your forgiveness, señora, though I do not think you will give it."

Santuva took a deep breath. "When the arm was falling towards me and I was pinned there, helpless, I thought about how stupid I had been. Giving up my life for coin— what a... what a *waste*. I thought of my son growing up without a father. My wife, alone. I would have died proud, but to what *end?*"

Beatriz looked at him. He looked sunken, withered some- how. But also at peace. Once she had hoped to see that look in the face of a different man. Tears blinded her. Beatriz had wept many times since that terrible day— in despair, in fear, in horror and pain. This time was different. She felt cleansed. This— *this* moment— had been why she had been coming. To see that it was possible. To stand witness to the moment a man redeemed himself— to see someone pass the test her Juan had failed.

When she spoke, it was to Juan, and not to Santuva. "I forgive you."

Santuva offered her a hand. "Come, señora. Ozzik cannot have gone far. Let me bring you home."

Auston Habershaw is a science fiction and fantasy author whose stories have been published in The Magazine of Fantasy and Science Fiction, Beneath Ceaseless Skies, Analog, *and other places. He also writes novels, his latest being his complete fantasy series,* The Saga of the Redeemed, *published by HarperVoyager and set in the same world as "The Puzzle Vault." He lives and works in Boston, MA and spends his days teaching composition and writing to college students. Find him on his website at aahabershaw.com.*

THE HAUNTED SPACESHIP

Jon Hansen

We found it
Way out past Neptune
A giant metal thing
Scarred by who-knows-what
A single giant door
Hung open and inside
I thought I saw
Something
Shift

It reminded me
Of the Simmons' place
Off Vanderbilt Road
Its cracked windows
Covering a dark stillness
I wasn't alone
In thinking this

The three of us argued about it
Claiming to be scientific
And rational
But really we were just
Playing chicken

In the end we settled on
Sending a robot probe
Just like we sent Jake Brodek's
little brother Tommy
To go on the porch
Push open the door
And go inside
Just a couple steps
We told him

We waited and waited
But the probe never came back
Just like Tommy

JON HANSEN (he/his) is a writer, librarian, and occasional blood donor. He lives about fifty feet from Boston with his wife, son, and three pushy cats. His short fiction and poetry have appeared in a variety of places, including Strange Horizons, Daily Science Fiction *and* Apex Magazine. *He can be found online at logicalcreativity.com/jon.*

HUMAN DNA

David McGillveray

Pierre Ledux bent over the projection of his new face, its icy blue reflection warped in the blank plastic curve of his faceplate, and made a series of tiny strokes with the beam of a light scalpel.

"I can never get it to look like how it looks in my head," he grumbled. "Can't get the eyes right, know what I mean?" He slouched back on his throne and set the pen aside, regarding his work critically.

"You've been fiddling with it for ages. Leave it alone, will you? It's fine," Gwynne told him. Her own face was the same one she had presented since she was quickened decades ago, unchanged by time. Unlike the rest of her.

She sat dwarfed in her own preposterous throne. In the Consensual, Pierre's living space appeared as a fabulous, but tasteless, receiving chamber in the palace of some ancient king. A huge log fire crackled impossibly in an airless grate. Sconces lit with glowing, fist-sized diamonds were bracketed to the walls and everywhere there was gold, coating the furnishings, the statues in their alcoves, even the floor. She felt like she was afloat in a molten pool of the dreadful stuff. The presence of Pierre's crèche-child propped upside down in one corner of the ceiling like a giant bug ruined the illusion anyway.

"Your tastes haven't changed," she said. "Unfortunately."

"There's nothing wrong with a bit of pizzazz, not in this drab corner of the universe," Pierre boomed. "I have to say I was surprised, and thrilled of course, to hear you were back in the Opposite. You've been away long enough to forget, if you weren't so unforgettable."

"Damaged engines. It took me years to get back to the Empire after Alb's accident."

"So you said in your message," Pierre said. "I was sorry to hear about the old rascal. I always liked him."

"Everyone did," she sighed, fingertips wandering to the brooch clipped to her utility belt.

"It must be costing you, paying those vultures on Ragana," Pierre mused. "You found something tasty out there, eh?"

"Stop fishing, Pierre. Let's agree it wasn't worth the cost and leave it at that, okay? So what's been happening in the old autocracy while I've been away?"

"Well, I'm still waiting for that fortune to drop into my lap for one thing. Never came quite as easy as I thought, that. Our glorious Halo Daniel, fool that he is, still believes the rubble ring is the last great human Empire rather than the shithole it actually is. The Transitional House have at least recognized this and remain intent on sending us all to oblivion. And the impoverished masses remain oppressed under the yoke of a cruel and indifferent system. So thinking about it, nothing's changed at all!" Pierre folded his hands over his middle section and laughed. "Oh, actually, there is one thing. Some crazy preacher has caused quite a stir among the outer Hours, daring to talk about possible futures that don't involve jumping blindly into trans-dimensional gates. He's obviously completely mad, but apparently he's pissed the House off to quite a considerable extent, so he can't be all bad. Apparently he carries his head around with him under one arm, imagine that!"

"The latest nutter selling hope, then. Hope never got me far," Gwynne remarked.

"Well you should take that up with the preacher. Speaking of which, I might have a proposal for you. That's why you're here anyway, right, to get back in the game?"

"I didn't say I wanted back in the game, Pierre. I just need something to keep me busy."

Pierre leaned forward. The unfinished facial projection glowed between them. "Come on, the Gwynne Tsang I knew was never interested in a *proper job.* I have something that's *right* in your line."

"No outsiders. We agreed," a voice cut in on the comms band, quiet and without inflection.

Gwynne started. She had forgotten about the boy. She looked at where he still clung above their heads. He wasn't looking at them as far as she could tell, wasn't even presenting.

"Don't listen to Auguste. He lacks context." Pierre craned his neck around and shouted, "You lack context, don't you, boy? This woman was pulling jobs while you were still random patterns swirling in the central repository! Back in the old days Gwynne here was a proper badass, weren't you?"

"I had my moments."

"And *what* a temper!" Ledux hooted. "You don't want to get on the wrong side of this one, Auguste, I'm telling you. She'll be a real asset, don't worry!"

In answer, Auguste unfolded himself, pushed off from the ceiling and sailed across the room with practiced grace, breaking the Consensual's illusion of gravity. The room's exit was rendered as a magnificent marble gateway carved with chains of stylized human figures. The boy performed a neat somersault as he passed through it and disappeared.

"Pay no mind, Gwynne, pay no mind. Only been out of the crèche ten years, doesn't understand the value of life experience. Enjoys a sulk, but he's a good lad. Gets things done."

"I never thought you had it in you, to be a donor," Gwynne said.

Pierre lowered his voice conspiratorially. "Truth be told it was a surprise to me as well. I don't even remember uploading the mental patterns. I was doing a lot of dizzies at the time, know what I mean?" He laughed uproariously. "You should've seen my face when the obligations notice arrived!"

Gwynne shook her head. "You going to tell me about this job then?"

"Right, yeah. So this preacher I was on about, apparently he's speaking at an event in a few weeks on Tenderness, you know, that artsy commune in the Eighth Hour. I've also heard that one of the neighbouring rocks, which just happens to be a House facility, has a stock of military grade repellers based on recovered Endless War tech. Top grade!"

When Pierre saw the interest projected in Gwynne's face and encouraged, he continued, "See, I told you it's your sort of gig. The best thing about it, though, is that due to the Transitional House's desperate desire to shut this preacher up, they're redeploying all their local security to capture the fucker! Which is when *we* will be making off with the goodies! Ha!"

Gwynne cocked her head to one side, considering. "Hmmm. Just like that. Where's your information from?"

Pierre was tinkering with his facial design again. "Can't divulge that, Gwynne, can't divulge. But it's good, I promise." He paused with the light pen held poised and looked at her. "Imagine how much that stuff's worth in the alternative economy."

"How many in your crew?"

"You would make us a magnificent seven. And I've got a fast rig lined up to whisk us into a substantially more comfortable future. What do you reckon?"

Gwynne sighed. "I wasn't expecting anything like this so soon. It's a bit heavy duty. I've been out of things a long time and I've got to think of Alb."

"Meaning?"

"Meaning I'll have to think about it."

Pierre opened his arms wide. "Well then, that's excellent! Can't ask for more than that. But don't take too long. I've got details to work out, and I need to know all the pieces in play."

Pierre made some final adjustments to his new face that only he could see and grunted in apparent satisfaction. At some silent command the face blinked out and reappeared projected over his faceplate. He now presented with a wide forehead and high cheekbones below young, innocent eyes. He tested out the synch with a few facial movements and then grinned widely with his new mouth. "How's that? I feel like a new man already."

"I've seen you wear a lot of different faces but somehow you always look the same," Gwynne said dryly. "Untrustworthy."

———◆●———

"Are you still in there, love?"

Gwynne peered through the thick glass of the clean room in the heart of the Ragana hospital facility where Alb lay strapped to a stone plinth. Since the last time she'd visited, Cordoza's team of psychotechs had opened up his chest to test his reactor. One arm had been removed, she didn't know why, and lay next to his torso like a discarded piece of tubing. They had also removed the top of his skull. She could see it floating in a transparent bag attached to the wall.

Wires led from machines into the componentry filling his skull, where, according to Transitional House doctrine, his human soul resided. Clamps held the silver spines of other instruments in place inside his head. Diagnostic displays on screens pinned above him seemed, to her unqualified eyes, unchanged since the last time she had come here. Alb had been locked away inside himself for twelve years.

Within the diffuse, largely outlaw region of the Empire known as the Opposite, Ragana was where you came for illegal chassis rebuilds, cerebral augmentations, sensorium enhancements and repairs following any manner of nefarious activ-

ities, no questions asked, money up front. But Ragana's psychotechs hadn't made any headway with Alb in all the months
he had lain here, said that they needed time to isolate the alien
code infecting his operating system. He needed further tests.
Always further tests.

"You must fix him," Gwynne demanded of Dr. Cordoza
when she had first brought him to the infirmary, exhausted
after years in space. "I can pay."

When the doctor at last understood what Gwynne was offering, the standards of care available were abruptly upgraded.
"Extraordinary," she said hungrily, examining the sample in
its protective case. She presented with a kindly, professionally
bland face, obviously cultivated for the job, but her manner had
quickly become all business. "Research rights on this sort of
thing are highly sought after. You *must* tell me if there is more
material. I can offer excellent terms."

"Is this enough? Can you help him?"

Cordoza nodded. "It's enough, but my team's resources ar-
en't unlimited. We'll try to flush the poison out but the infection, the *infiltration*, inside your husband's systems, it's Endless
War era technology, much smarter than our own. We'll want to
proceed very cautiously."

One look at Alb still lying there, as lost to her and inert as
ever, and Gwynne had set aside any thought of joining Pierre
on his lunatic venture. Ledux had been a pro back when they
were starting out, but now he just seemed desperate, and desperate meant risks would be taken. She'd been a fool to even
consider it, a selfish, dangerous part of her craving something
to make her feel alive again. "I'm old, Pierre. My priorities are
different. I've got to think of Alb. I'm sorry, but I know you'll
understand. I hope things work out."

She would be here for Alb, should he wake.

The prize she had brought back from the hinterlands, a
fragment of which she'd used to satisfy the psychotechs, should

have set them both up for life. Instead they both existed in different types of limbo. She cursed the day they'd entered that system, prospecting for relics from the past.

She placed both of her hands against the glass and held herself there, braced in the planetoid's microgravity. It was just all so hard.

"Are you still in there, my love?"

———————•◦•———————

She remembered pulling Alb from inside the asteroid, his face-plate blanked and his body lifeless in her arms, that *thing* breaking free.

The system's distant sun, a spark in the void, offered no comfort. They hung in space for a long time, drifting in the debris field, Gwynne unable to rouse herself to action, over-whelmed by fear, by relief and by grief. She stared at the point where the ancient human warship had disappeared, so arro-gant and cold, dismissing their lives as if they were nothing.

Eventually she signaled to the rig waiting a few kilometers distant. The simple vehicle, a boxy scaffold of superceramic pipework and struts open to vacuum, nosed up to them like a worried pet. Gwynne settled Alb as best she could in the com-mand nest, a spherical space cluttered with the paraphernalia of a long life lived together. The little personal touches in their living space, the jaunty banners and other decorations she had hung from the rig's beams, now seemed silly and empty of meaning.

Her immediate instinct was to get as far away as fast as possible, but she fought her emotions down and set to scanning the rubble left when the ship, with their unwitting help, had broken free. It was a long shot, but there had been something else in there that had also survived the millennia. If she could locate it, their prospects back in the Empire would be consid-erably improved.

Gwynne synched her mind with the rig's senses and spent hours calibrating and recalibrating her equipment, tuning it to chemical signatures she guessed were relevant. Various organic ices within the rocks muddied her results and she investigated dozens of false indications before finally spotting a telltale flash of green in the readouts projected onto her inner eye.

She separated a personal rig from the bulk of the main vehicle, little more than a cage with a control column and a tiny engine, and nudged it cautiously into the debris field. A rain of dust and grit began to patter off her plastic hide. She steered around larger chunks of rock, using gravitic repellers to push obstacles from her path, zeroing in on the signature while scanning real space with her visual senses set across as broad a spectrum as she could process.

And then she finally sighted it. She recalled the silvery sheen of the ancient suit worn by the human warrior, untarnished by the millennia spent frozen to the hull of her feral former ship. It drifted there: a forearm, still in its gauntlet, severed just above the elbow, vacuum frozen but still containing a trove of cellular material, from the distant time when humans were made of flesh.

———————————•◦•———————————

Halo Daniel had sat at the head of his Empire for two hundred years. The imperium comprised a belt of rubble billions of kilometers in circumference orbiting in the baleful red light of Eye, the system's star, and was part of the galaxy-spanning legacy of devastation left by the fleshies and their Endless War. The ring was divided into the twelve Hours of the ancient human clock with the Opposite in the sixth Hour, as far distant from the influence of Farasito, the Empire's capital world, as possible. Before she had taken up with Alb and set out as a prospector, Gwynne had spent much of her life in the region, where a loose agglomeration of misfits, crooks, dissenters and malcontents spread over a few thousand worldlets were linked together by a mutual mistrust of imperial authority.

And so here she had returned. Marquesa was a hollowed out rock like any other, a manufacturing center for all sorts of goods exported across the Empire, most of it illegal. Gwynne had used it before, either as a base or a place to pick up transient work, and still knew a few people from decades past. It had been enough to get her in past the vetters, ever-suspicious of infiltration by Transitional House moles or imperial cops. This time she had chosen it for its proximity to Ragana, a few thousand kilometers distant.

Gwynne took a job readying laymen, semi-autonomous intelligences fitted into empty human chassis, in one of the big factory complexes close to the centre of commerce that was the Mouth. "Your psychotechs on Ragana mixed the spirits for me, so they should be decent," Berto, her new boss, told her. She vaguely knew him by reputation as a fair sort. "I've got a backlog of about a hundred and fifty units, so we need to get cracking. Let me know when you're ready for another mind and I'll download it from the mini-crèche."

"No problem."

Gwynne and Alb had used a pair of similar units for years. They were highly illegal in the Empire where animating human bodies, the supply of which was already tightly controlled, with anything other than an officially blended human spirit would have been a blasphemy if the Transitional House ever admitted to being a religion. After the physical fitting of the brain-unit, Gwynne tutored the fledgling intelligence in virtual, integrating it with its physical chassis and working through an extensive palette of control and response patterns. It was decent enough work, even satisfying to see each new layman come online and ready itself. Demand for the robot workers was pretty steady and Berto paid her well enough.

Truth be told, she needed the work to establish some sort of new normality for herself. Half the time she felt she was being crushed under some unimaginable weight, that her reactor was sputtering its last, like she couldn't live at all. When, a few weeks later, Berto asked her if she'd be interested in taking on a team of her own, Gwynne declined. "No thanks. I'm here for the monotony, not the promotional prospects."

"You need to think about yourself, Gwynne, for the long run," Berto counselled her, backing off quickly when her temper erupted. He was only being kind, but she wasn't ready for kindness.

Gwynne spent the off-periods between shifts either making the trip to Ragana or brooding in the bare cubicle she had rented deeper inside the asteroid. She spent long hours staring into the brooch she kept as a keepsake, watching as the series of images of Alb and herself cycled through, over and over, floating before her like ghosts.

She pulled back the privacy screen of the cubicle ahead of another evening spent like all the rest and was disconcerted to find a scrap of waste plastic stuck to her room's utility hub. She snatched it up and immediately went to check the strongbox she kept in the back of the big locker that filled one wall. For such a den of rogues, the culture within Marquesa was not one where petty crime was rife, but nevertheless Gwynne felt a momentary panic. Satisfied the locker and box were untouched, she looked at the fragment in her hand. Scratched into the plastic was an invitation:

Meet at The Core? 2200. P

Pierre. She wondered what trouble he had got himself into this time.

Plenty, as it turned out.

————◦•◦————

The Core was Marquesa's liveliest social spot, situated deep inside the asteroid's guts. It was a large, vaguely spherical bubble strung with a webwork of wire ropes to which were attached dozens of meeting nodes like droplets of condensation. The dark holes of tunnel entrances dotted the walls, busy with a constant flow of people. Clumps of power cables and fibre optics were pinned haphazardly to walls and litter floated everywhere, especially the coin-sized discs of one-shot dizzy viruses.

In Consensual, the place was transformed with political murals and animated cartoons parodying Halo Daniel and his court of dimwits. Screens showing a dozen entertainment and news feeds flickered from walls and ceiling, depending on your physical orientation, and holos and advertisements danced. The common band was filled with the pulses of chime-muzak and the babble of voices.

Gwynne clung to a hand-hold inside the Core's main entrance and scanned the crowd. There must have been over two hundred people in, a big crowd for Marquesa, filling the three-dimensional space, clinging to the nodes at all inclinations, many of them buzzed on dizzies.

She was pinged on her private band. A familiar tone with a familiar tag. "Don't you recognize me, then?"

She craned her neck and peered into the crowd again. Finally, she spotted a figure waving at her from thirty meters away and launched herself towards it.

"Another new face, Pierre?" Gwynne said, joining him at the spherical node and gripping its supporting cable.

"I like a fresh look, you know me."

This time, the face he presented was older, with small eyes and a thin nose and mouth. It had a pinched look about it, not his usual style at all. Gwynne could tell he was high from the way he held his body, drifting outwards from the node, fidgeting. "You seem fresh enough," she observed.

"You my donor, now?" He made one of his dismissive gestures. "Thanks for coming, Gwynne."

"Why wouldn't I?" But it had occurred to her in uncharitable moments that it might have been a mistake to get back in touch with him in the first place. He'd always attracted complications.

"I thought you might have heard."

"No. I take it, though, that the elusive fortune continues to evade you. Come on, Pierre, stop stringing it out."

His facial projection momentarily glitched. "Well, you know that job I told you about? It didn't quite go to plan."

"You'll notice I don't look shocked," Gwynne said. "What happened?"

"That damned preacher never showed up, on Tenderness. Changed his plans or something, which well and truly fucked ours. There was a full complement of security in attendance when we came knocking at that House facility. It was bad, Gwynne, really bad. I barely got away, the rig got shredded. Had to leave most of the crew behind, unfortunately." Pierre was twitching now, becoming more animated as he told the story. He kept jerking his head to look everywhere about them, as if he was expecting trouble.

"Only you got out? Shit."

"Just me and the boy. I'm finding myself desirable for all the wrong reasons. I think the Juntii are hunting me. In fact, I know it. One of the others would have talked. *I* would, if the Juntii were asking."

"You think the *Imperial Guard* are after you?" Gwynne was incredulous. "What *was* this place you were trying to turn over?"

"Never mind, never mind, a mistake, in retrospect. It's done now. First thought was back to the Opposite, to find some friends. I guessed you might be in Marquesa."

"How far down your list was I?" she said sourly.

"Don't be like that. I'm short of friends just now, you see, and I have an urgent desire to take a long sabbatical in the outback, just like you and Alb did. But I do need a bit of advice and some, er, seed capital to get me started. It'd be like an investment, know what I mean?"

Gwynne scowled at him. "Berto point you in my direction? I'll bloody kill him," she said. "How much do you think I'm making fitting out laymen?"

"Leave it out, Gwynne. You basically told me you came back from your adventures with something of substantial resale value." Pierre was becoming agitated now, rolling his head from side to side. "You can help me out, can't you? I'm in deep shit here."

"I can lend you a few hundred, but that's it."

Pierre reached out suddenly and grasped her forearm. "I think you've got more than you're letting on. You always kept something in reserve, I know you."

"Take your damn hand off me, Pierre," she hissed, and he snatched it back as if electrocuted. "I'm looking out for myself here. No one else is. *You're* not. I've got my own fucking problems."

"Alb's *gone*, Gwynne. You should accept it. You can't do anything more for him."

"What do you know about it?" Gwynne shouted, suddenly furious. "Why do I have to care about your shit, anyway?"

He quailed and his perpetual bravado abruptly left him. "Please, Gwynne."

She almost broke. "Not this time, Pierre. Sorry."

"That's twice you've turned me down," Pierre said, trying to force a joke. His face glitched again.

Gwynne pushed away from the node and headed back the way she had entered. When she turned to look back, Pierre was still hanging there alone. After a moment she saw him take something from his belt and snap it into the hard-linkage umbilical port in his neck. A shudder run through his body. She shook her head and left.

———•◦•———

A shift with the laymen, the same lonely trip to Ragana, longer and longer periods in fugue, that null state where awareness was dialled down to almost nothing and time passed unnoticed. She knew she was shutting the world out, enclosing herself in her own bubble of unhappiness.

A further invasion of her privacy shocked Gwynne from this sinkhole. She pulled back the screen of her cubicle to find it in disarray. Her few belongings drifted about the place in a tangle; all been given rough treatment. An embroidered gilet Alb had once given her for special occasions was ruined, its many pockets torn away.

"Fucking Pierre."

The man must have finally run out of options, or dizzies.

The locker stood open, everything inside thrown out. Gwynne made a quick search, already knowing that the strongbox would be gone. She cursed herself for her stupidity, for not doing enough to keep the relic safe, for forgetting its importance to both of them, for being so preoccupied. Everything returned to sharp focus.

She rushed from the room and pulled herself rapidly down drab, unaugmented corridors.

She pinged Pierre and issued a series of macabre threats. There was no response.

She contacted Berto. "You've seen Pierre Ledux around, right? You know where he's staying?"

Gwynne headed towards the Mouth. Berto had seen Pierre talking to some of the dockers there a few times. She was acquainted with some of them herself, people who had helped her with her rig when she had returned to the Opposite. Pierre, the idiot, had not been particularly discrete. A few enquiries gave her a cubicle number in the dockworkers' accommodation district.

When she arrived seconds behind a further barrage of furious pings, she thumped at the door-screen. It was locked but the door was flimsy plastic and it didn't take her long to force it open.

Her rage dissipated as she inched into the darkened space, instincts tingling, the room across her visual senses. The cubicle was carved direct from the rock of the asteroid, bigger than her own, enough for two people to share. A utilities and entertainment hub in one corner blinked on standby. She accessed it and brought the lights up. Pieces of plastic shrapnel drifted above a long, stone table wrought from the stone.

For one crazed, vertiginous moment she thought it was Alb lying there, strapped down in the infirmary, and she cried out. But it wasn't Alb. A tiny maelstrom of neon pixels, remnants of Pierre's final face, swirled above his faceplate in randomized patterns.

The violence of it was shocking. His body was covered in deep dents from the repeated impact of some blunt, heavy implement. One foot had been methodically beaten until it came away at the ankle. The fingers had been smashed from each of his hands. The thick plastic of the chest casing that protected his reactor was cracked in multiple places, fragments flaking away. His skull was caved in.

Gwynne went over to him, drifting above the body, but couldn't bring herself to touch it. She knew he was gone. "Pierre," was all she said for a long time. "I'm sorry."

Finally, she shook herself and made a search of the room. The strongbox wasn't there, of course. She transmitted a memory-recording to Marquesa's security core and left in a hurry.

Inside the Mouth, dockworkers, repair crews, arriving and departing traders and laymen went about their business, sailing in freefall across the great cavern in what to the untrained eye looked like a chaos of crisscrossing trajectories, fleeting mid-air crashes and near misses. In reality, it was a complex, coordinated, even graceful ballet. Or that's what your average Marquesan would tell you.

The Mouth opened directly into space, its circumference studded with gantries and repeller stations like flattened pyramidal teeth, manipulating incoming craft in shaped gravity fields and preventing collisions. Larger vehicles were either tethered to the asteroid's surface or sat in parking patterns outside, while inside the cavern were utility huts, mountains of stacked cargo containers, berths for personal transports. A dozen species of lumpy machinery crouched on the rock floor, supporting the various activities of Marquesan commerce.

Gwynne asked around but no one had seen anything more unusual than usual, and had not seen the individual she described. In the mean time, her own conviction grew as to where she must go next. There was only one place in the Opposite to go to with a preserved human arm.

Gwynne's rig was a much-diminished version of its former self. She had sold off or simply discarded sections of the superceramic scaffolding that made up its structure and stripped it of much of the junk she and Alb had accumulated over the years. It was parked on Marquesa's skin a few hundred meters from the Mouth, looking like the abandoned skeleton of some minor structure as yet unfinished.

She quickly checked over its simple systems, released it from the pitons driven into the rock and pushed away from the surface using its repellers. When she was far enough out, she reoriented the craft and engaged its much-repaired engines, building acceleration slowly and heading for Ragana once again.

———————•◦•———————

It was most of a day's journey to the hospital world. She usually made it on automatics and sank into traveller's fugue, but she was too wired for that. She sat on a crossbar at the front of the rig and stared out into vacuum, bathed in the accusing red light of Eye.

The frenzied viciousness of Pierre's murder had appalled her. The Empire contained and sometimes fostered the full complement of human wickedness, but that level of violence, of uncontrolled fury was almost unheard of. It was easier for her to be angry than to think about the way she had left things with her friend.

The Transitional House, those self-appointed arbiters of imperial morality, warned against the horrors of human history, of the incalculable ruin their forebears had inflicted upon the galaxy. They taught that the remnants of humanity that held on should look only forwards, to forge their own future excised from the destructive patterns of the past. Despite the House's many doctrinal insanities, the unfulfilled promises of opening gates to other universes and transitioning towards some undefined but glorious future, this core tenet had always made some kind of sense to Gwynne. Who in their right minds would want to live in a universe where whole suns could be extinguished just because someone disagreed with someone else?

Nevertheless, there was something deep within the modern psyche that could not fully set aside its fascination with what life must have been like when human minds were encased in soft flesh, when they were masters of the galaxy and all its energies. There were countless worldlets scattered through the Empire filled with communities of archaeologists, historians, mystics and alchemists dedicating their lives to scratching the itch of racial memory. They sought remnants, artefacts, memory and data from the millennia piled high behind them. They looked backwards with as much fervor as the House put into telling them they must not. Gwynne and Alb themselves had made a living from this obsession, selling the fragments of the past they found amongst the rocks and empty spaces of the hinterlands, the tightly packed and equally ruined star systems neighbouring the Empire. The ultimate grail for these delvers in history was a strand of human DNA, the base building block of human flesh and mind. If they could have that, might they then understand their gods? Might they rebuild the glories of the past, only without the mistakes? Might they bring them back?

Gwynne had felt this longing, this hunger, rolling out of Dr. Cordoza when she had first shown her the finger she had cut from the ancient human's hand. To Gwynne, it was just an artefact, something rare and important and valuable, but still just a thing. But to Cordoza and others like her, it was the source material of human existence, a possible gateway back to a more fecund past. She would have given anything for it.

As the rig approached Ragana, still invisible to her own senses but picked out clearly in the displays the rig's systems projected into her inner eye, Gwynne pinged the doctor.

Finally, there came an answer. "Yes? Miss Tsang?"

Without preliminaries, Gwynne said, "Has anyone approached you or any of your staff recently? With something like what I gave to you?"

A pause. "There was someone. A little while ago."

"Did he identify himself? Was there a transaction?" Gwynne asked.

Another pause, longer this time. "That's not your business."

"It bloody well is my business. What he has was stolen from me."

"You told me you didn't have anything more," Cordoza accused.

Gwynne thought that for someone involved in the profession of healing, Cordoza was a particularly mercenary creature. "That's because I lied to you, doctor," she said. "What do you take me for? If you lot knew what I had I'd never have been left alone. Don't deny it, you know what I mean. We can do business again if I recover it, okay? So has there already been a transaction or not?"

"There hasn't been a transaction," admitted the doctor. "He refused to show it to me so I sent him away until he changed his mind. He's still on Ragana."

"Did he use the name Ledux?"

"No, he was anonymized, didn't transmit an identity signature. He wasn't presenting either."

"Yeah, that's him." Gwynne felt fear and relief in equal measure. *He hasn't been able to open the box*, she thought. She had to get to him before he did anything stupid trying to get inside. She also wouldn't put it past Cordoza's crew to take matters into their own hands if she didn't get to Auguste first.

"Can you keep him there?"

"I told him if he could fulfil his promises he'd be rich. I don't think he's going anywhere. Look, I can locate him for you but whatever business you have with each other, you'll have to resolve yourself. Just don't damage the material."

"Your priorities are clear, Cordoza," Gwynne said.

She had made the approach to Ragana dozens of times but never at anything like this velocity. The irregular lump of rock and iron that was Ragana rushed from the darkness and, in an abrupt change of perspective, transformed from just another tumbling worldlet into a sheer wall of imposing grey rock careening towards her. She applied reverse thrusters and repellers both and brought the rig in to the closest docking bay to the location Cordoza had given her.

———————•◦•———————

She pinged him directly. She put out a call on the common band. She tried to access him through Ragana's central comms net, but he either wasn't listening or was blocking incoming signals.

Gwynne followed the schematic of the asteroid in her mind's eye, pulling herself along side tunnels, through better lit thoroughfares and communal spaces alive with consensual reality. Like many worlds in the rubble ring, Ragana had been hollowed out piecemeal, gnawed through with no coherent plan. As she made her way inwards, tunnels opened out at random to dormitories and factories, workshops, stores and laboratories. Later, as it had begun to specialize in research and medical treatment, more and more of the spaces had been adapted by the psychotechs to their new functions, their walls painted white and dotted with screens. Gwynne felt outside the flow of others' lives, seeing the business of the medical community carrying on around her as though through a foggy lens as she drew closer to her target's location.

One of Cordoza's people identified himself to her at the node where three residential tunnels met. He clung to a wall with one hand, a large-caliber projectile gun gripped in the other.

"The doctor said you had first dibs," he said. "The door's tagged in ultra."

"Has the place been cleared?"

"You have him all to yourself, for now."

Gwynne nodded and moved past him. As promised, a secure-looking metal door two hundred meters along one wall had been daubed with a flash of ultraviolet paint.

She pinged him again. When there was no response she put all her strength into thumping the door. The anger and tension in her had grown such that the vibrations could have been felt half way down the corridor.

Finally, a channel opened. "Get lost."

Oh yes, it was him. She remembered the tone.

"Hello, Auguste."

After a pause, he said, "You're the one with the dead husband."

"He's not dead," Gwynne grated.

"That's not what Pierre said. As good as, is what he told me."

"Before you killed him, you mean? I saw what you did to him. You're a monster."

"I didn't like you the first time we met, miss badass old timer. I thought you were all mouth," Auguste jeered. "But you're here, I'll give you that."

"I'm glad you're impressed."

"Impressed? No."

Into this new silence, Gwynne said, "You've got something of mine. Can't open it, though, can you?"

"If I'm not interrupted further I'm sure I'll get there."

"Do you even know what it is?"

He gave what might have been a laugh. "I do. The thing about Pierre was that he was always talking. Jabber, jabber, jabber, on and on, never stopped. But sometimes it could be useful, all that talking, and me having to do all that listening. He knew people here, and he knew you had dealings here. A bit of chat here, a bit there, you know how he was. And there you have it. That's medical confidentiality on Ragana for you. So you see, I do know my business and I know what it is, you patronizing bitch. And now you're going to help me open it."

The selfish, arrogant, murderous little bastard. "You're out of your mind."

"Pierre didn't do things the way I wanted them done and that was bad for him, but you still can. We can split the proceeds and both go away satisfied, no?" Auguste said.

"Why would I trust you with any sort of deal?"

"Who's talking trust? Don't believe in it myself. But self interest, that you can trust."

"Give it up, Auguste. You won't get away from here. Pierre was my friend," Gwynne snarled.

"Sure I can get away. All the medics care about is the DNA. Anyway, you weren't such a good friend to Pierre, were you? Knocked him back when he needed help. Not so friendly, that."

"You understand nothing," Gwynne hissed. She pushed herself away from the door and down the corridor, moving rapidly. "The only help you're getting from me is this."

Gwynne unlocked the activation code buried deep inside her memory and transmitted it with a thought. The door of Auguste's hiding place exploded outwards and impacted the tunnel's opposing wall on the end of a gout of flame. The detonation sent a shudder through the fabric of the asteroid.

She may have been remiss in securing the strongbox itself, but not what was inside it. The small but potent charge she had booby-trapped the box with obliterated it entirely, along with Auguste Ledux and a not insignificant section of the surrounding residential units. It reduced to atoms the gauntlet on the hand of a human who had lived cased in flesh four thousand years before, along with Gwynne's hopes for the future.

Sirens began to blare on the common band. She kept going.

———•◦•———

Gwynne pressed her hands against the glass. They had taken Alb's body away an hour before but she hadn't moved.

"After the, ah, incident, Ragana's authorities are pushing for a resolution to your situation," Cordoza had told her. She had at least made an effort to look apologetic, but the message was clear: Gwynne was out of credit. "We've tried everything but the infection is still inside his mind. Every time we try and flush it, it reconfigures itself. I hate to admit it, but it's beyond us."

"I understand," Gwynne replied numbly. Now she was here, at this point, she felt exhausted, so tired she was almost unable to feel anything at all. Perhaps a part of her had always known it would come to this. "I'm out of options."

"Not quite," Cordoza said, her manner softening. "We can shut him down completely. Who knows what we might be able to do in the future? There's enough left in your account to store him. If that's what you want."

"In purgatory?" Gwynne mumbled.

"People sometimes come back."

Gwynne nodded absently. "Store him. Yes, do that."

At last she turned away from the window and returned to her rig. She unclipped the brooch from her belt and opened its polished black lid, cycling through the floating images of Alb and her together. "My little box of keepsakes," she whispered to herself.

Deactivating the picture-show, she pressed points on the brooch's inner and outer casing in a particular sequence so that a tiny compartment opened up behind the holo mechanism. Inside it, sealed between tiny slivers of glass was a cell sample, a scraping of human DNA, so that she could continue to exist.

David McGillveray was born in Edinburgh, Scotland but now lives with his family in London. After a long period of silence, lockdown started him writing again and this story is one of the results. His fiction has previously appeared in Interzone Digital, Kaleidotrope, Space and Time, *and is forthcoming in* Shoreline of Infinity *and* Analog.

AMATEUR MYCOLOGISTS

Mariel Herbert

I. Primordium

They tried and failed the old fashioned art of folding
their dreams into clean sheets, compulsive threads.
Turned their depressed light sensitive stems
  parasitic.
Burnt matches.

Ovate friends advised from orthodox toadstools.
He learned to stalk her cycles, perennially confused
that a broken veil meant go. Twisted deceivers.

Then came the specialists with polyporous forms,
collecting fluids and words. Inorganic contamination.
One night he clicked 'buy' and waited for a miracle
herb that never sprouted. She sought out healers.
Witches in black forests. Hens of the woods.

In the end they had moonlight and sporophores. Both
pressed wood ears to the earth, let themselves
  compost
for a time. They poured out blue wine, consumed
oysters warm and cold. Brown and golden they fused
together in a fairy ring the usual way: umbonate to
umbilicate. Mating like lobsters.

The starched couple slept on midnight ground
  primed
by amethyst thunderbolts, dampened with
  desperation.
Flawless substrate for fruiting. They needed,
needed her to open up her angel wings and fly.

Thus they shared with their magic mushroom child
ignoble destroying rot. Amanita, good girls hide
their gills beneath their caps. Beware bleeding
toothed pigs hunting moon night truffles. Stay
safe as a hedgehog in winter.

II. Release

Such puffball parents, to pom-pom false morals
at their child's margins. This mycelial girl isn't
a fawning chanterelle; not their mirror yeast,
their sweet-bred unicorn. No, she's an earthstar.

A rhizomorph. Blue runner.

And so she grows. Grows up. Spreads out with a
  swish
of those hyphal tips. When her parents try to find
  her
old fruitbody, she's already packed up and gone
underground. Filamentous.

Her new found family's common and communal
symbiotic and intimate: all love, infinite strings.

SINBAD THE STAR CAPTAIN

Sarina Dorie

Ace Vader
Period 2
The Great Gatsby Essay

Sinbad the star captain sat on the bridge of his state-of-the-line battle saucer, the *U.F.O. Flying Dutchman*, listening to the distress signal coming from Omega Centauri 9. He stroked the scar on his jaw with a scaly, purple hand and squinted at the view screen with all three eyes, trying to make out the image of his colleague in distress.

"Help! The planet is under attack! Our fleet can't hold him off. The Great Gatsby is at it again," the other captain's voice said through the static.

"We are on our way," Sinbad told the captain of the *U.F.O. Titanic*. He nodded to the ensign at the controls. "Hyperspeed 10."

With the technology the Great Gatsby had stolen from the Delta Aortronians, an entire planet could be turned into Swiss cheese using magnetized space particles. Wherever he went, the Great Gatsby left a path of destruction in his wake.

Sinbad exited the bridge and went to his conference room. He pressed the button on his intercom. "Lieutenant Hashiba, Commander Mariyama, I need to discuss tactical plans with you."

Lost in thought, Sinbad stared out the porthole at the stars streaking past. He remembered his hatch-parents and grandparents on his own home world on Andromeda 3. He would have been happy to embrace the peaceful way of life as a farmer or furry Torb herder like his ancestors, but instead he had been destined for greatness. As the son of an interstellar crime lord, his childhood had been a battleground of events that left him scarred inside and out.

When a great solar flare had unexpectedly destroyed much of his world, the United Peace Battalion sent out rescuers to search the planet's remains and brought aid to those who needed it. With his hatch mother, little sister and grandparents dead, all Sinbad had left was his crime lord hatch father.

Sinbad's only chance at a normal life was to escape the tyranny of his father. He hid in a suitcase of another survivor to be smuggled off the planet. At any moment he knew he could be discovered. He prayed to his ancestors, promising that if he could escape, he would only do good for the universe. He would fight evil and put an end to arms dealers and crime lords like his father.

His ancestors must have been listening because Sinbad found freedom.

In his new colony, he no longer lived as a prince, but was just another refugee. Humans made snide remarks about his purple skin, accent and three eyes. At the space academy, Sinbad learned that instructors expected more from Andromedans and he had to work twice as hard to earn the respect of humans.

On his ship, it was no different. He noticed the way his first officer sneered at his every remark as they discussed tactics. What did he have to do to earn the respect of these humans?

At a speed of hyperdrive 10, it only took an hour to arrive at the battle. By the time they arrived at Omega Centauri 9, the destruction had been complete. The fleet of U.F.O.s looked like Swiss cheese.

"Too late again!" Sinbad said, collapsing into his chair in defeat.

A dead two-headed Orionian floated by a porthole. One of the ensigns lost his lunch next to the console. Green edamame beans floated in the putrid, yellow puddle. The bridge filled with the smell of vomit.

Unlike some of the previous planets they had found, this one was still intact. Instead of being torn apart, the planet was charred and scarred. Sinbad's two hearts started to pound. He'd seen this before. The planet looked like his home world after the solar flare.

His throat as dry as a dead Torb's dung, Sinbad barely managed, "Hashiba, hail the planet. See if there is a response. Yamimoto, scan the planet for survivors. Analysis of the planet?" Sinbad had a sinking suspicion he knew what the science officer would say.

Ensign Yamimoto read the computer's findings. "It looks like a giant solar flare has killed off most of the planet's population. Our readings show there are a few small pockets of survivors."

Sinbad nodded. He thought of his own childhood. The flare had been a blessing and a curse. He stood. "Ready the away teams. We need to provide medical attention to those left."

"But captain, aren't we going to go after the Great Gatsby?" Commander Mariyama eyed Sinbad's purple skin with disdain. "We must avenge our dead comrades. In the name of the United Peace Battalions, we must hunt down that warlord and make him answer for his crimes."

"No, we must help the living," Sinbad said. "And we must discover the link between the Great Gatsby and these great solar flares. I've seen destruction like this before. It can be no coincidence."

To be continued. . . .

Grade: F+
Ace,

   Although the mechanics, grammar and skills of your writing exceed the 10th grade writing standards, it does not meet the criteria of the assignment. How does this essay remotely relate to the Great Gatsby other than you naming the villain Gatsby? Furthermore, I'm sure the physics in this story is impossible. Next time read the directions. And possibly pay closer attention in your science class too. Please review the original directions for the Great Gatsby essay.

   Also, use your real name on your essay so I can give you a grade. I do not know which of my students goes by "Ace."

   Mrs. S

———————•◦•———————

Directions:
Students, write an essay about your first day of school. Remember, you are being graded on grammar, mechanics and clarity of ideas. Today we are focusing on the Common Core English Standard for high school students: Produce clear and coherent writing in which the development, organization, and style are appropriate to task, purpose, and audience.

~~Ace Vader~~ *Steven Nakamura?*
Period 2
The First Day of School

   Sinbad the star captain told the search parties, "If this is anything like my home world, Omega Centauri will be affected by a series of after-flares. It's important our crew stay suited up and assist the survivors to safety."

Sinbad dressed in his radiation-resistant suit and heaved a case of medical supplies onto the transportation platform. The chief psychic onboard the *U.F.O Flying Dutchman* sent Sinbad the star captain and three crewmembers to the planet side by telekinetic powers with other away teams to follow in other locations.

On the planet, Sinbad took in the seared remains of blackened corpses. His away team split up, using their advanced technology to find those who remained. Some of the Omega Centaurians were so charred, he couldn't even recognize them as humanoid. One thing he did recognize on the planet was something that it had in common with his home world: evidence of interstellar gangs. The armored space cruisers of weapons dealers sat in ports, caught unaware by the solar flare. He found slaves chained together, the metal collars burned into their skin.

Flashes of memory from his own home world jolted through Sinbad like an electric current. This destruction was too much like reliving his past. His stomach churning, he forced himself on. He had a mission. He was here to rescue those in need.

The bodies inside the dwellings were less damaged. These humanoids were small and gray. Their large white eyes stared up unseeing.

Sinbad's life form locator blipped, alerting him that life was near. In the subterranean dwelling of a home, he found a wrinkled old alien sitting in a corner, looking so peaceful and calm he wanted to believe the alien was asleep. The alien rested next to a tub of water. At the bottom lay a smaller figure. Unlike the others, her skin was the scaly purple of an Andromedan like himself. Her diminutive frame and the opalescent sheen to her scales reminded him of his little sister, now long gone. She wore a slave collar. Another mark of the interstellar black market. Etched into the collar was the crest of the Great Gatsby.

The child had probably drowned in the tub during the solar flare. Tears filled his eyes. The injustice of it was too much. His life form locator beeped. Someone was still alive nearby. He scanned the room, pausing at the bath tub.

The life was faint and fading. Sinbad pulled the small figure out. He placed a technologically advanced breathing mask over the slave's face which expelled the water from her lungs and pushed air in instead. The child opened all three of her black eyes and sat up. She was alive!

It must have been the water that had protected her from the radiation of the solar flare. But how could she have held her breath so long? He could hold his breath for half an hour at most, but the solar flare had occurred at least two hours before. This ability was far more like the Moldovian fish people than his race.

There was something more to this slave than met the eye.

The little girl smiled and hugged him. Sinbad had saved one life.

He hadn't won the war against the Great Gatsby, but he had won a small battle.

To be continued. . . .

Grade: F+

By process of elimination, I am guessing this journal entry was written by Steven Nakamura? Is that correct? If so, please put your REAL NAME at the top of the paper so I can give you credit. Also, it would be helpful if you followed the criteria of the assignment so I can give you credit. You are putting so much effort into your writing. If only you would put that effort into your actual assignment. You are a good writer. I want you to pass my class. Please, help me help you. Do the assignment that is as-

signed. Redo this essay and turn it in again and I will not count it late.

Also, it would be a nice touch if you didn't leave my class halfway through so that I didn't have to give you another detention.

Mrs. S

———————•◦•———————

Steven Nakamura a.k.a. Ace Vader
Period 2
Redo: The First Day of School

My first day of school was when I lived back in Japan with my parents and little sister in an apartment half a mile from the subway. In Sapporo, the city where we lived, it was common for kids to walk to the subway and ride it by themselves. I know it is different here in America, but that's the way it was there. I used to walk there with two neighbor girls and we rode to the school together. If we goofed around and were late, we would get hit with sticks by the principal. We were only late once. That was on our third day.

I hear they don't do that to students these days, but I don't know since I haven't been back to Japan and don't know anyone there anymore.

I don't actually remember the first day of kindergarten or much from the first couple weeks except being hit by teachers if I gave the wrong answer or displeased them. The only real memory I have of kindergarten was the second or third week when a stranger came into our school. I knew something was wrong as soon as he stepped into my classroom, but not for the reason I should have. I didn't even notice the knife in his hand. I kept staring at his shoes. He wore outside shoes and had tracked dirt down the hallway and onto the train track floor mat in my classroom.

Only a madman would wear shoes inside.

The students next to me whimpered. Yamaguchi Sensei ran toward the intercom but the man overpowered her and stabbed her in the chest. Kindergarten students screamed. I might have screamed. I don't remember. I sank under my desk and closed my eyes. Even with my eyes closed, I kept seeing crimson blossom unevenly across her white blouse and drip onto the crayon drawings stacked on her desk.

Sometimes I still see the blood when I close my eyes.

"Everyone just stay quiet and no one is going to get hurt," the man said. He stood in front of the door. No one could get out.

Some of my classmates were running around, some huddled together in the back, and some hiding under desks like me. One girl was wailing especially loud. He kept telling her to shut up, but she wouldn't. He slit her throat.

Someone threw up next to me. I remember whole edamame beans floating in the putrid, yellow puddle.

I watched him stab three more classmates before I jumped out the window. My classroom was on the third floor. I broke my leg and hit my head. I must have passed out for a couple minutes. When I woke, I lay in the bushes, in too much pain to do more than cry. The police arrived a couple minutes later and stormed into the building with their batons ready. Guns aren't commonly used by criminals or police in Japan, so there was no gunfire. After the madman was apprehended, the school was evacuated and children sent home in a bustle of noise. No one heard me whimpering for help.

The school's janitor found me three hours later.

Grade: C+
Steven,

Good job following directions this time! Your writing is clear, coherent and well-organized. You definitely meet the content standard for your grade level. I just want to check in with you about some of the information you mentioned in your essay. Was this all non-fiction or did you make some of it up? Did your school really have a stabbing? I looked on Wikipedia and it said Japanese police officers carry .38 revolvers. I am seeing holes in the facts of this story, just like I did with the science in your Sinbad story. I need you to submit non-fiction.

By the way, please use only your real name on your classwork.

Mrs. S

Directions:

Students, write an essay about your favorite holiday or family celebration. Remember, you are being graded on grammar, mechanics and clarity of ideas. Today we are focusing on the Common Core English Standard for high school students: Write narratives to develop real or imagined experiences or events using effective technique, well-chosen details, and well-structured event sequences.

Steven Nakamura
Pen name: Ace Vader
Period 2
Christmas with the Nakamuras

Christmas is not a traditional Japanese holiday and many people at home in my native country don't celebrate it except as a novelty. My mother didn't want to celebrate it because we were Buddhist and she didn't like the commercial aspect. My father thought it would be cool and trendy to show off to his friends that he could afford expensive gifts for his family, which is why we celebrated it. When I was seven, I asked "Santa" for a Star Wars video game. My mom thought it was too violent and worried it would cause me to have nightmares again like I had after the school stabbing, so she asked my dad not to get it for me. He did anyway.

I played it out in our family room as they fought about it in the kitchen. Although the size of our apartment in Sapporo was considered palatial there, it would be considered very small and cramped compared to an American home, and sound travelled easily through the thin walls. When I heard my father slap my mother, I flinched and pretended I didn't hear. I heard her scream and ask him to stop and I heard another smack. I started shaking so hard I couldn't play the video game. I was scared for her. I remembered how bruised her face had been the last time he'd beaten her.

I didn't know what to do, so I woke Obaasan—Grandma—from her nap and told her what was happening. She shuffled along with her cane. I kept tugging on her arm to hurry, but she only moved at one speed—extra slow. I tugged on her sweater. She shooed me off. In doing so, she lost her balance. She fell and broke her hip.

I tried to tell my father that Obaasan was hurt, but he punched me in the head and called me a liar. I fell and smacked the side of my face on the corner of the traditional Japanese table that was in our kitchen. I didn't realize until later that I'd cut myself.

My father smelled like sake, so I knew there was no point in talking to him. I called 1-1-9, our emergency rescue number. An ambulance came. Not only did Obaasan and I have to go to the hospital, but the paramedics made my mother go to the hospital, which shamed her when people saw her abuse. My father beat me when I came home. He smacked me so much, my stitches opened where the doctor had sewn up the side of my face from when I'd fallen down. It left an angry red scar that ran from my jaw to my cheekbone.

Grandma died two weeks later from an infection she got in the hospital. My father said that was my fault.

My mother felt so humiliated that everyone knew what an unhappy marriage she had that she tried to throw herself in front of a train. It didn't actually kill her. It dragged her along the tracks for miles. People told the driver they heard someone scream and the police had to come to take her to the hospital. My father laughed and said my mother couldn't do anything right. She couldn't even kill herself.

I hated him more than ever. I hated her too. I hated everything about my life.

While my mother was in the hospital, I asked her why she put up with him beating her. I asked her why we couldn't just go out to the country and live with my other Obaasan and Oji-isan and hide from him. She told me that if she tried to leave, he would come after her with his friends from the Yakuza and kill her. I didn't understand what the Yakuza was. Years later, my aunt told me that the tattoos on his arms and legs that he kept hidden marked him as a secret Japanese gang member.

That was the only Christmas we celebrated. We celebrated many Japanese holidays like New Year's Day, Obon and Golden Week but those holidays weren't much better.

Grade: A+

Steven,

Good job meeting the Language Arts core standards again. Your English is so proficient, I didn't realize you used to live in Japan until I read your school records. I called your adopted mother today and had a long discussion with her about you. It definitely sounds like you have had many interesting and difficult life experiences before coming to America. She confirmed your stories are real. I apologize for my previous comments.

Let me know if you need anything. I am available after class if you ever want to talk.

Mrs. S

———————•‖•———————

Directions:

Students, write an essay about your favorite childhood memory. Remember, you are being graded on grammar, mechanics and clarity of ideas. Today we are focusing on the Common Core English Standard for high school students: Produce clear and coherent writing in which the development, organization, and style are appropriate to task, purpose, and audience.

Steven Nakamura
Period 2
Favorite Childhood Memory

It's really hard to come up with a favorite childhood memory. The most memorable times involve someone getting hurt or dying. There was the tsunami that hit Otaru while we were visiting family, there was the time Ojiisan was supposed to be watching my baby sister in the bathtub but he fell asleep and she drowned, the Yakuza mob boss who shot at my father, but hit my mom and uncle instead, and the time my aunt dressed as a man and smuggled me in a dog carrier onto the train so no one would recognize her when she kidnapped me and brought me to the airport in Tokyo. I think she must have paid someone to give me a passport as her child. She's never been clear on that detail.

My aunt tries to help me think of happy times, but sometimes, no matter how hard I try, I can't do it. She tells me the bad things that happened when I was little aren't my fault. There are days I almost believe her. Often I ask myself what I could have done differently on that first day of kindergarten. Should I have ran out the door while the madman was stabbing my teacher? Should I have let him slit my throat so I wouldn't have to live through everything that followed? Some days I wish he had.

Aunt Tamami says to focus on something that will make me happy. Nothing makes me happy. Except *Star Wars, Star Trek*, aliens and spaceships. I want to be somewhere that isn't on this world. I like writing about space adventures because that's the one time I'm not me. Sometimes in my stories I can make bad things into good things. This is the only time I can make good things happen.

I wish I knew how to make good things happen in real life.

Grade: A+

~~Steven~~ *Ace,*

> *Good job meeting the English core standards again.*
>
> *I'm glad you came and talked to me after class and told me about some of the things that are stressing you out. I haven't observed your peers treating you differently because you are Japanese or teasing you and calling you scar face, but I will be more aware of side conversations from now on and will intervene when I notice these situations come up. You are so quiet in class sometimes I don't know if something is wrong, so it was good for me to be aware of what was on your mind. I want to help you if these incidents come up again. I like your plan to grab a hall pass and take a walk if it gets too hard to concentrate and to leave me a note if you don't feel like you can directly tell me what is going on.*
>
> *As far as our next assignment goes, ignore the directions on tomorrow's essay. Finish writing your story about Sinbad the Star Captain. We both need something happy to think about. Show me how you can take something bad and make something good happen.*
>
> *Mrs. S*

Directions:

Students, write an essay comparing and contrasting your life to various characters in *Catcher in the Rye*. Today we are focusing on the Common Core English Standard for high school students: Write informative/explanatory texts to examine and convey complex ideas and information clearly and accurately through the effective selection, organization, and analysis of content.

Ace Vader
Period 2
Sinbad the Star Captain: The Adventure Continues

Sinbad sat in his conference room with his officers, listening to their report. He was the only Andromedan. All of the others had the dark hair and smooth, fair skin of humans. Izumi, the science officer was genetically engineered to have a third eye like his but she lacked his purple scales. Out of all of them, he suspected she might have understood him the most. Lt. Hashiba had the gray pallor and diminutive build of an Omega Centaurian but he had hair and never spoke of his alien ancestry.

No matter where he was and what he did, Sinbad always felt like an alien.

"Good news, Captain. We have determined that the solar flares were indeed caused by the same weapon that makes ships into Swiss cheese. The only difference is it was aimed at the planet's sun instead. Something must have gone wrong. The weapon wasn't intended to be used that way."

"Theories?" Sinbad asked.

His chief science officer shrugged her shoulders. "We can speculate that the space invaders intended to use it as a weapon against the fleet, but missed and the polarized particles were aimed at the sun instead."

"Or they aimed it there on purpose, knowing the intended affects," Sinbad said. "Status on the refugees?"

The intercom beeped and the communication officer on the bridge announced, "Captain, we are being hailed. Another distress call from a nearby ship. We're twenty minutes away at hyperspeed 10. Should we proceed?"

The expectant faces of his officers waited for him to reply.

Sinbad stood. "Tell them we are on our way. Commander Mariyama, ensure all survivors of the solar flare are onboard in the main cargo bay in the next five minutes."

His officers began to argue. Sinbad walked out on them. He wondered if they would dare question a superior had that superior been human.

Needing answers before he faced more of the Great Gatsby's wrath, Sinbad took the turbo-elevator to the cargo bay where the solar flare victims were being treated. A small group of purple-skinned Andromedans like himself flocked to him when he entered the bay. The slave that resembled his late sister hugged him around the waist.

"Ani!" she cried, using the word for "big brother" in their native language.

His heart skipped a beat. He told himself this wasn't his sister. The opalescent scales and shape of her three black eyes were a coincidence, nothing more. But he couldn't quite believe it.

"Imoto," he simply said, the name for 'little sister' in his own language. "I must ask you some questions. You wear the crest of the Great Gatsby. Have you met your owner?"

Her smile faded. "He isn't my owner. He's my creator."

"What do you mean?"

"I am an experiment. A clone. Years ago, when the Great Gatsby tested his stolen weapons on his enemies who were about to discover the experiments he'd been funding, he lost both his planet and family. A charred smear of my DNA was all that was left. He took that miniscule amount and recreated me. He rebuilt me—only stronger." She glanced at the other children in the cargo bay. "Out of all his experiments, I am his favorite. I am the one who will make a perfect soldier to follow in his footsteps. I am the one he will stop at nothing to retrieve."

A shiver stole over Sinbad. Alive again, this was his sister. This conversation had raised more questions than answers. All he knew was that he had to stop the Great Gatsby.

————————◆•◆————————

Sinbad resumed his position on the bridge. The vessel they approached in no way resembled a Peace Battalion U.F.O. as the distress signal had claimed to be. He rubbed at the angry line that scarred the right side of his face.

The battle cruiser drifted, life support running. It had sustained damage to the engines and pieces of the shields were gone.

"Hail the ship," Sinbad said.

"No response."

"Should we board?" Commander Mariyama asked.

"No. My captain's intuition tells me this is a trap. Have our telekinetic transport an android over." If Imoto was correct, they had something the Great Gatsby wanted. This was the first step in a deadly game with the crime lord.

"Yes, sir. The alien vessel is scanning our ship. I've raised our shields and the scan has been cut off." Lieutenant Hashiba said.

After a few seconds, his security officer reported, "The droid has been blown apart."

The cruiser before them flickered to life, engines powering up, shields unfolding and covering the naked hull of the ship.

"Catastrophic power source located on board, sir. Sub atomic particle magnets aimed at us!"

Sinbad shook his head. Even knowing it was a trap, his opponent had gained the upper hand. Or had he? The Great Gatsby had no psychics onboard for telekinetic transportation. If he wished to retrieve his prize, he would have to board. Sinbad was counting on the Great Gatsby wanting to retrieve his genetic experiment more than destroying the evidence she existed.

"Lower our shields. See if that gets his attention," Sinbad said.

"Sir!" Commander Mariyama stood. "I cannot—"

"Do not make me repeat that order. Time is of the essence." Sinbad's three eyes narrowed. "Anything he aims at us is superior to the technology we possess to deflect it. Our only chance for survival is to let him see what we have."

"Incoming message on screen," the communications officer said.

The screen displayed the bridge of the Great Gatsby.

"I have searched my entire life for you, Gatsby. At last we meet in person."

In the captain's chair sat an Andromedan. Spikes had grown around his brow ridge, a common sign of age. His purple scales had faded to red and pink, the uneven pattern over his face and neck resembling elaborate swirls of water. Still, Sinbad would have recognized the other man anywhere. His two hearts pounded and his vision swam.

The Great Gatsby appeared just as surprised. His three eyes widened at the sight of Sinbad and then he smiled. "At last, we meet again."

"Again?" one of the bridge crew asked. They gave each other confused glances.

It made sense: the solar flare that had been a way to cover up evidence of his genetic crimes, the clone of his little sister, the crime lord that had started it all with the first solar flare.

None of these details had been a coincidence. It had only been a matter of time before Sinbad discovered the connection.

"So after all this time, you've become a captain. It doesn't surprise me. You were always destined for greatness." The Great Gatsby leaned back with satisfaction. "You've thirsted for power. You have your own ship and your own minions to control. How does it feel . . . son?"

"I am not like you. I am not your son," Sinbad said through clenched teeth.

"Oh, but don't you see? You are, only hiding under the name of the United Peace Battalions. Surely working with humans can be no joy for you. Wouldn't you rather be working with your own kind? Wouldn't you rather have the respect you deserve than serve humans who treat you with contempt and disgust? Can't you see? They don't respect you. They tolerate you. These humans don't understand us."

Sinbad glanced at his subordinates, noticing the way they avoided his gaze, either ashamed to find out his tie with the crime lord, or ashamed that the Great Gatsby's words rang true.

The Great Gatsby leaned forward. "You and I aren't so different. We both thirst for the same things. Perhaps we can come to a compromise."

Sinbad glanced at his bridge crew staring at him open-mouthed. "Perhaps. But not here. Not like this. We must meet in private."

A smile twisted the Great Gatsby's lips. The link cut out. That was all the convincing his father needed to allow him to teleport onboard. His crew was a different matter.

Commander Mariyama snarled, "I hope our psychic loses you in space, you traitor!" It took two officers to hold him back.

"That's enough, Mr. Mariyama. You are relieved of duty." Sinbad faced the wide-eyed stares of his crew. "As I said before, do not make me repeat an order. Time is of the essence."

Sinbad armed himself with a laser gun, security restraint net and homing device. "Keep a frequency open between myself and the ship."

Lt. Izumi studied Sinbad with all three eyes, seeing something deeper than the commander's suspicion. "Captain, do you require backup?"

"No, this is a mission I must do alone. Be prepared to get the *Flying Dutchman* out of here if the Gatsby tries anything."

He stepped onto the tele-transporter pad in the corner of the bridge. Within seconds he was on the bridge of the enemy vessel. He and his father were alone.

The Great Gatsby, old and feeble, rose on shaky feet. "You have something I want. Surely you know what it is."

Sinbad nodded. "My sister. Your weapon."

"Yes, and now I have you. My true heir. We will rule the universe together. But first, you will bring me your sister."

Instead of casting his eyes down in subservience, Sinbad met his father's gaze as an equal. "It doesn't have to be like this. You can hand over your weapons and assume a new identity. You can give up crime and take up a life of doing good."

His father laughed. "Surely you jest."

"Show the universe that Andromedans can be heroes. Show humans our people are more than tyrants and thugs," Sinbad said.

"Never! You will hand your sister over to me!"

Sinbad threw the security net at the Great Gatsby, knocking the old man over and trapping him within. "By the power of the United Peace Battalion, you are under arrest."

The Great Gatsby roared, "Computer, self-destruct!"

A high-pitched whine filled Sinbad's ears. The panels on the far wall blinked red. That couldn't be a good sign.

"You think you've won?" the Great Gatsby asked. "Think again. I'm not going without a fight."

"Your days of causing interstellar terror have come to an end," Sinbad said.

"If you're so certain, have it your way then. It was nice knowing you." The Great Gatsby's voice turned into a maniacal laugh.

The lights on the panels blinked more quickly. The high-pitched whine grew into a buzzing throb. The communication screen exploded in a shower of sparks. A wave of noxious gases boiled over them. Sinbad ducked away from the heat. A brilliant light engulfed him before everything went dark.

———•◦•———

Sinbad gasped cool, clean air and opened his eyes. He sat hunched over on the transportation pad. His ears still rang and his skin felt raw. Stars streaked by the porthole as they travelled away from the Great Gatsby's vessel. The exploding ship on the screen commanded the attention of all eyes on the bridge.

"You did it! We've won!" Lt. Hashiba said.

The crew released a chorus of cheers.

Sinbad should have felt happy about his victory, but instead his two hearts weighed heavy. This time he had won the war, but he had lost his father in the process. A father he wished he could have changed.

"What next, captain?" Ensign Nishida asked.

There was still so much to be done: medical attention for the survivors of the solar flare, giving his cloned sister a normal childhood, and of course, writing up his report on the incident for the Peace Battalions. Most of all, he remembered his vow: he would fight evil and put an end to arms dealers and crime lords like his father.

Sinbad pulled himself to his feet. "Who's the next interstellar crime lord we should go after?"

To be continued. . . .

Grade: A+

*Good job, Ace! I can't wait to read the next install-
ment of Sinbad's adventures. Now that the Great Gatsby
is gone, who will Sinbad's next opponent be? We are doing
a unit on* Catcher in the Rye. *Any chance you can work
that title in to the next story?*

Mrs. S

Sarina Dorie has sold over 200 short stories to markets like Analog,
Daily Science Fiction, Fantasy Magazine, *and* F & SF. *She has
over ninety books up on Amazon, including her bestselling series,*
Womby's School for Wayward Witches.

*A few of her favorite things include: gluten-free brownies (not
necessarily glutton-free), Star Trek, steampunk, fairies, Severus
Snape, and Mr. Darcy. She lives with twenty-three hypoallergenic
fur babies, by which she means tribbles. By the time you finish
reading this bio, there will be twenty-seven.*

*You can find info about her short stories and novels on her web-
site: www.sarinadorie.com*

TADPOLE

Nicholas Jay

Duty done, favor won. That was the law, in those days.

Every morning, the Fisherman and the Shipwright arose and prayed before their altar, exalting the Visionaries for blessing them with bountiful sun and wind. They trawled their nets across the lake, then traveled to market where the Visionaries' magistrates would reward them with food, fiber, and their masters' continued favor.

A simple, dutiful life. No room for deviation or dissatisfaction.

The sailors' good favor ended one morning when panicked, raspy screeches shook them from their customary pious trance. They rushed to the lakeshore to find a hideous infant water-breather, yowling and flailing about in the muddy shallows.

Before the Fisherman could protest, the Shipwright scooped the vile creature in his arms and waded into the chilly lake so it could breathe.

"Get out of there," the Fisherman hissed. "What if more are nearby?"

"They never come so close to shore," replied the Shipwright, unusually distant.

"Yet you hold one. It's dangerous."

His admonitions rang false in his own ears. The sailors had endured countless water-breather attacks during their fishing voyages. They knew well the jaundiced glow of their half-moon eyes, their sun-shy skin, the sucking sounds they made when above water--fearsome features masking slow minds.

This small one looked nothing like that. Its eyes were white and docile, its skin a pearly pink, mottled with grey-green freckles. Strangest of all was the translucent film, thinner than a dragonfly's wing, loosely covering its face.

"He's harmless," said the Shipwright, straightening out wrinkles from the creature's mask. His touch was delicate, despite his thick fingers and calloused hands. Like all of the Shipwrights, he was bred for the trade: barrel-chested, brawny arms and shoulders. Though they had known each other many years, the Shipwright's tenderness still caught the wiry Fisherman by surprise.

"We must send it back. The Visionaries would declare it an abomination."

The Shipwright nodded, slack-jawed and glassy-eyed. "Best to do as the Visionaries do."

He waded back to shore and passed the creature to the Fisherman. It chirped happily, intrigued by the new face. Now its noises were melodic, peaceful as evening birdsong. The Fisherman imagined the lake at twilight, the sky emblazoned with orange and violet stripes. He sat on the dock next to the Shipwright, their toes tracing ripples in the water...

The creature began to cry again and the image vanished.

They boarded their catamaran and set sail. Far from shore, the Fisherman held the screeching creature by its ankle and dropped it, returning it to the depths where it belonged.

———•◦•———

Later that day, the Fisherman was cleaning the morning's catch when sharp cries interrupted him again. The same water-breathing thing lay beneath the dock, screaming itself hoarse.

He was alone now; the Shipwright had set sail to test repairs he had made to the catamaran's pontoons. Wincing, the

Fisherman rescued the screaming imp from the shore and waded into the lake, submerging its face below the water. Its desperate wails changed to satisfied mewls.

It spun in place clumsily, riding the lake's gentle waves and
grabbing onto the Fisherman's body to steady itself. He found
he didn't mind being an anchor for the little thing. As they
played, he became mesmerized by its peculiar features. Its eyes
radiated innocence and its skin glowed against the murky lake.
Every time it pawed at his arm, warmth swelled in his chest
and cheeks.

"Who could you be?" he asked. "Tadpole, I'll call you."

The child stared at him with ebullient eyes and the Fisherman again was swept away by daydreams. He imagined the
Shipwright concealing his face behind a blue kerchief, the
same one the Fisherman had sewn for him years ago. Then, a
dramatic ripple of fabric, the Shipwright yelling "peek-a-boo!"
and Tadpole collapsing into a fit of giggles...

"What are you doing?" The Shipwright's gruff voice sounded from above him.

"He came back to us."

"How long have you been here, idle?"

The Fisherman bristled at his accusation. "I have been
minding--"

"Today's catch? Your duty?"

The interrogation ended the Fisherman's reverie. He noticed the sun hanging low in the sky. The winsome creature
now seemed monstrous, its skin marred by grey-green pox, its
papery mask shriveled and mildewed. Even its once-soothing
voice abraded his ears.

"It is an abomination," the Fisherman droned.

"Best to do as the Visionaries do," sighed the Shipwright.
They shuffled aboard the catamaran to banish the creature
once more.

When they returned at sunset, the day's catch had spoiled. Their first breach of duty in months.

———————————•⦁•———————————

The Visionaries issued their reprisal that evening, sending furious storms to batter the lake. The Fisherman and the Shipwright knelt before the altar to pay penance in kind. Lash after lash, they poured penitence down their own legs and backs.

Amidst peals of thunder and grunts from their own tortured ministrations, the familiar sound of coarse cries pushed through the rain to assault their ears for the third time that day.

They looked to each other, their gaze taut as rigging for a straining sail.

"We must take him in," said the Fisherman.

"We cannot," scolded the Shipwright.

"But you felt it, didn't you? When you carried him?"

The Shipwright's face fell. There was no denying it. Within them both, a timid flame had been lit, a tiny brightness casting images, happy and hopeful, onto the walls of their memory.

"Tell me," whispered the Fisherman. "What did you see?"

"It doesn't matter," snapped the Shipwright. "He--it--has no place here. It is an abomination--"

"He is a child!"

"You would so quickly forsake your duty for that thing?" The Shipwright sighed and laid his strong, gentle hands on the Fisherman's shoulders. "I cannot watch you bring yourself to ruin."

The Fisherman studied the Shipwright's solemn eyes. The child's peals grew louder, filling the space between them.

"I forsake nothing. Tadpole will do so much for us. You'll see."

The Fisherman pulled away from the Shipwright, following Tadpole's cries through the heavy rain. His wounds stung and his body ached, but when he picked up the child, a familiar warmth spread through his chest.

They waited beneath the dock, bobbing in the bay's gentle water, until the rain weakened and the moon hung high. The Fisherman smiled as he carried Tadpole to the house. He would reacquaint him with the Shipwright, show him his grace and the tenderness of his touch.

But the house was dark and quiet, candles snuffed and windows closed. Left behind on the Visionaries' altar, the Shipwright's blue kerchief lay crumpled and forgotten.

In the days that followed, a new Shipwright came, identical to the departed one: barrel-chested, brawny arms, every movement imbued with measured tenderness. He kept his distance from Tadpole at first, but as the days went by, he warmed to him just like the Fisherman had.

Together, they sat on the dock at twilight, their toes gliding through the water as Tadpole swam confident circles around them. They played peek-a-boo with a new kerchief--an orange one--the Fisherman had sewn. They curled up in bed, Tadpole between them, wearing the water-mask they made for him.

But the flame inside the Fisherman, the one Tadpole had kindled, faltered without the tender gaze of the old Shipwright. Though the new one looked the same, the Fisherman felt nothing when they touched.

Nicholas Jay is a conservation-minded urban planner living in Atlanta, Georgia. His work has appeared or is forthcoming in Metastellar, The Dread Machine, Hyphenpunk, and Tree and Stone Magazine, among others. He enjoys his time most with either pen, violin, or map in hand — sometimes all three at once. Find him on Twitter and Instagram at @kn1ckkn4cks.

Remorse, A Love Story

Sean Shapiro

I reached the climax of my vignette, a ribald number about a couple who happen to run a brothel in their basement looking to match their daughter up with some pious schnook, and everyone was gleefully agog and aghast. Everyone except this sullen yeshiva bocher.

'Maggid,' he said, with not even the dust of civility in his voice, 'do you *ever* regret telling a story?'

The room went quiet.

I chose my answer carefully. I said: 'There are times, yes, I'll admit. But—and this is a principle by which I live—while I may regret telling a story, I never have remorse for having told it.'

The bocher was not much impressed by my answer. 'Is that *supposed* to sound clever? Aren't regret and remorse just fancy ways of saying the same thing?'

'No, boychik,' I assured him. 'They are very different creatures, in ways that only a very fine and perceptive mind can apprehend—though to a genuine *chochem* those little details loom as large as the Leviathan. Nu, I'll tell you a story that'll illustrate it far better than any long-winded *drosha* from me ever could ...'

It happened some time ago in Vilna that there was a man, a certain Sender Rosenberg, who loved his wife Pearl with all his heart and all his soul. And it happened that Pearl loved him back, loved him deeply, very deeply indeed. But it also happened that she loved her children more, far, far more than her husband.

And her youngest, Jonas, she loved most of all.

His hair was tawny and lustrous, his eyes penetrating, his teeth perfect, his body lithe, his movements graceful. Heads turned (men's as often, though not as openly, as women's) when he sauntered down an upmarket boulevard. Painters and sculptors offered him gifts and money to pose for them. He had charm, wit, poise, the voice of an angel. And when the stage (nu, how could it be otherwise with his gifts?) became his vocation, he performed to nothing less than rapt admiration.

His performances drew the crowds and the cognoscenti. And no one attended more performances than his mother, Pearl. Nor did anyone do more to keep Jonas in the limelight. When the budget was blown, when the sets were ruined by fire or water, when the censors threatened to cut a pivotal number and the moralisers wanted to shut the show down for good, it was Pearl who found the funds, Pearl who furbished the sets, Pearl who placated the fuddy-duddies.

And who provided Pearl with funds, connections and influence?

Her husband, of course. Her immensely wealthy husband, Sender Rosenberg, who loved her with all his heart and all his soul.

How it happened Sender was never quite sure, but suddenly he was paying the salary of a theatrical manager to book and produce plays for his son and hiring a talented young playwright, a certain Lukas Melnikas, to write the leading roles that best encompassed his son's range. It wasn't long before Lukas and Jonas were collaborating on cabaret tunes and droll monologues of their own devising and not long after that they were sharing a house (rent courtesy of Sender) in a most bohemian part of town, collaborating on their art late into the night or, indeed, any time inspiration struck, and their friendship blossomed and bloomed until it wasn't long before Lukas was as frequent a weekend and holiday guest in Sender's home as his own son, Jonas.

They were discrete, of course. But their desire burned as brightly as their love and one balmy summer night, like Abimelech king of the Philistines who just happened to look out his window and catch Isaac 'frolicking' (as the Torah puts it) with the woman he claimed was his sister, Sender just happened to wake up with a pain from belly gas and en route to relief, passed his son's bedroom and heard the unmistakable sound of Jonas and Lukas 'frolicking'.

The next morning Sender took his son aside and spoke to him in private.

The young man was outraged and upset. 'Never! Never! Never!' he shouted. 'Never see him again!? How can you be so cruel, Father?'

Sender maintained his composure. It was important that his son understand the consequences of his attachment to Lukas—he could lose his audience, his liberty, his physical safety.

'And what if (Heaven forbid!) your mother should find out?'

The blow was not quite as devastating as Sender expected. Jonas merely shrugged. 'We hurt no one,' he said. 'Mother will understand when I explain.'

At this, Sender lost his composure. The truth of the matter was—as Sender well knew—she would. Pearl would most definitely understand her son's feelings. 'Not another kopek, not another loan or a favour', he bellowed, 'will you get from me if this goes on!'

'We make enough on our own these days, thank you very much,' replied Jonas.

Many more words were exchanged that morning, many of them intemperate, but before they parted, Sender softened his

tone and said: 'Promise me, Jonas; promise me you won't say a
word of this to your mother.'

'I don't want to hurt her, Father, but I don't want to make
promises I can't keep either.'

'Promise me,' Sender hissed.

'No, Father.'

———————◆◆◆———————

'You look like a herring somebody left out in the sun,' said
Abba Karpinovitch.

'Huh?'

'Your face, it's all grey and pasty. Plus, you haven't heard
a word I've said. Nu, tell me, boychik.' The grizzled racketeer
paused to light Sender's cigar. 'Is this *tsoris* on your shoulders
also my *tsoris* or is it a private *tsoris*?'

'Private, Abba.'

Abba nodded knowingly, opened the bottom drawer of his
capacious writing desk, withdrew a bottle of the good stuff and
two glasses and plonked them on the table. Pouring generous
measures, he said: 'You wanna talk about it?'

Sender's pained expression intimated otherwise, but he ac-
cepted the proffered glass and half a bottle later he was telling
Abba his troubles.

'I hear what you're saying, Sender. But listen, you're going
about this completely the wrong way.'

'I am?'

'You're wasting your breath on the boy. He'll grow out of
it soon enough. Meanwhile the more you *bak* him about it, the
closer you drive him to his little bird, hmm? Anyway, Jonas
isn't the one that needs a good talking to.'

'What do you mean?'

'I mean when a certain someone visits another certain
someone with a nice bundle of notes and a nice new set of lug-
gage and a one-way train ticket to Minsk or Pinsk or Moscow
and leads him to understand that leaving town would not only

benefit a person's financial situation but would also be good for his health and wellbeing, that's what I mean.'

'Maybe not this time.'

'Why not this time? What's so different about this time?'

'I know the lad. He's not a bad boy.'

'Suddenly you come down with scruples?'

'This isn't business. It's a matter of ... of the heart.'

Abba scoffed. 'It'll be a matter of disgrace. For the whole family. When it comes out. And the way they're carrying on it will come out, believe you me. Do me a favour, take the favour. Disgrace's no good for business. Yours or mine.'

Sender did no more than wince.

'So that settles that,' said Abba.

<hr />

Days later Menachem paid Sender an unannounced visit.

Menachem was one of Abba's 'boys' (as Abba called them), a hulking fellow with a lumpy face and an air of surly hostility. Not bothering with petty preliminaries like 'hello' or 'good afternoon' he said, 'I could do with a thank you and a *l'chaim.*'

'For what, Menachem?'

'Saved you a bundle, didn't I?' He smiled a jagged barracuda smile. 'Also, that *sheigetz* will never touch your boy again.'

'What are you on about, Menachem?'

'I paid the degenerate a visit. Lucky for me he was at home.'

'What d'you mean home?'

'The one your son shares with his little bird.'

'You went to my son's *home!?*'

'Nu, where else? Don't worry, don't worry. They're flaky as Greek pastry, these artist types. The pigs'll have no trouble cooking up a motive.'

'My God, what have you done?'

But he knew. Somehow, Sender knew.

The brute had never met his son, didn't know Jonas from Adam.

He didn't wait for Menachem's reply. He fled his office, ran straight to his coachman, ordered him to speed to his son's home.

His corpse was hanging from a cord in the drawing room.

A sheet from a recently penned score with the words 'Forgive me' written across it in an over-deliberate hand had been placed just-so beneath his dangling feet.

———————•|•———————

A maelstrom howled in his head as he turned his back on his son as he plodded out of the house as he instructed his coachman to summon the police as he awaited their arrival; as he watched them lower his son like an overthrown occupier's flag as they covered his boy in a blanket; as they searched the house as they opened chests and drawers as they riffled closets as they tore pages from notebooks as they read private letters as they fished out smutty pamphlets, forbidden books, dirty postcards and bespoke sexual paraphernalia from their hiding places as they asked him question (What possessed you to rush over like you did? Was it a premonition or did you have concerns about his state of mind?) upon question (How do you suppose Jonas received those fresh bruises on his arm? Are they marks of love or violence, do you think?) upon question (Did you know about your son's, er, proclivities? Where is the other young man who lives here—Lukas? Had he and Jonas had a falling out, a fight? When did you last see this Lukas?) and suddenly the howling was not in his head alone. It was coming from outside the house, coming from the street.

And he knew. Again, he knew. Knew what the wailing was. His wife.

He ran. Ran careless of consequence from his interrogator, a sour plainclothes inspector. But by the time he reached the street outside the howling had stopped. She was on the ground. She'd collapsed from emotion and could not be revived.

A doctor was sent for.

There was nothing to do, he said, but wait.
And hope.

───────◆◆───────

Lukas they found early the following morning hanging from a
tree in Rasos Cemetery. He had a note in his pocket. The note
read, simply: 'Forgive me.'

Nu, it happened that it was convenient for the Authorities
involved to close the case and call it a murder-suicide.

So they did just that.

───────◆◆───────

Abba paid Sender a call on his third night sitting shiva.

It was long after *Maariv,* long after the last visitor had left
that he turned up at Sender's front door. He came alone.

'I know everything,' he said to Sender. 'And I've taken care
of everything.'

He pulled a cheque from his pocket. 'This isn't for what
was done. The guilty party has had more than a taste of the
world-to-come. You needn't worry about that. No one will ever
hear from him again. No. This is for Pearl—she should have
a *refuah sheleimah.* Take it, use it to bring her back to health.'

The cheque was considerable. Sender spent it all. Down to
the last rouble. He spent it on doctors, specialists, wonder rab-
bis, folk healers, mavens of every sort and stripe, quacks and
charlatans of every colour. Nothing worked. Pearl remained as
she was. She ate, she drank, she performed her body's functions. But she wouldn't open her eyes.

───────◆◆───────

A year passed and on the night of Jonas's first *yahrzeit,* the
first anniversary of his death, there came in the dead of night a
knocking on Sender's front door. Half-asleep, he rose from his
bed and shuffled to the door. He hadn't seen his visitor for a

year, and he almost didn't recognise him from the way his flesh had rotted since.

'This,' said Menachem, handing Sender a letter written on parchment, 'is for Pearl. Take it, use it.'

Sender read the letter. The characters were Hebrew, but the words made no sense to him. They were not Hebrew nor Yiddish nor Aramaic nor any language he understood. When he looked up from them the shrivelled corpse wrapped in a shroud of shadows was gone.

The letter, however, remained.

———————•◦•———————

No one could tell him what it said. Oh, plenty people claimed they knew what the words were. They claimed that they were written in the language of the Chaldeans or the language of demons or that it was in a code they could crack or some other tall story. But nothing of what they told him ever rang true. He paid them their consulting fee and he sent them on their way. And then he consulted the next maven, and the next, and the next, and the next ...

———————•◦•———————

And then one day, quite by chance, he happened to be riding on a train and sitting opposite him, head stuck in a volume of Talmud, was Rabbi Kalman Spektor, the famous *Dokshitzer Chochem*.

'Excuse me, rabbi,' said Sender, 'but might I bother you for your opinion on a matter of life and death?'

'You put it like that—I can say no? Nu, how can I help?'

Sender handed him the revenant's letter, saying nothing of the circumstances under which it had come into his possession.

Rabbi Spektor read the letter from beginning to end.

'It's no language I know or recognise. But it's not entirely meaningless.'

The letter, he explained, was written in several cryptic codes and the keys to these codes were contained in the body of the letter. These keys—acrostics, transposed letters, puns (in Hebrew, Yiddish, and Aramaic), allusions, quotations, and so on—were all drawn from the book of Kohelet. He cited examples but, lacking an intimate knowledge of Solomon's book of wisdom, Sender could make neither head nor tail of the rabbi's methodology. (And quite frankly neither can I, your narrator, no matter how many times it is explained to me.)

'If I paid you for your time, rabbi, would you be able to tell me what it says?'

Three days later the rabbi summoned Sender to his home.

'It's a hoax,' he declared.

'Are you absolutely certain, rabbi?'

'Nu, what else could it be? For a start, it claims to be written by a demon.'

'A demon?'

'For want of a better word. Claims to be an agent of temptation with the power to influence the world of men. Claims to be able to cure your wife's sleeping sickness if you follow his list of instructions.'

'And what are his instructions?'

'Superstitious nonsense.'

'Please, rabbi. You must tell me exactly what the letter says.'

'Here,' said Rabbi Spektor, handing over his notes, 'read for yourself.'

'If I do as it says here,' said Sender, 'he'll reveal himself to me?'

'If you do as it says,' the rabbi prophesied, 'you will do nothing to improve your wife's situation.'

Sender did exactly as the letter asked.

He obtained the required incense. He picked and plucked the required plants, and he desiccated them in the required manner. He purchased the required animals. And he killed them all himself in the required manner. And he turned their skin to parchment. And he wrote the required names in the required ink on the parchments. And he burned the parchments and the dried plants and the pungent incense in a specified vessel in a specified manner at a specified time saying certain words.

And the demon gave him a sign: footprints in the ash he sprinkled at the foot of Pearl's bed, rooster-like claw marks that meandered across the carpet ...

He followed where they led—a door opposite the bed. A door that had never been there before. The door was closed. Sender knocked.

'Come in, come in,' said the demon.

———————•◦•———————

He was only terrible to look at if you weren't looking directly at him. When you were looking directly at him, he was a gentleman of nondescript features in a crisp business suit with a few peculiarities (thumbless hands, talon-like fingers, rooster-like feet, pupilless smudges where his eyes ought to be) that marked him as not of this world. But when you caught a glimpse from the corner of your eye ... well, then he was a roiling of maggots in meat, squamous lesions turning black and splitting, bones splintering, wounds suppurating, entrails spilling, tumours blossoming, flesh suffering and expiring. He was the nausea in the pit of your stomach when the doctor delivers his prognosis. In a velvet-on-skin voice he thanked Sender for the offering and its pleasing aroma.

'Thank you for granting me an audience, my lord,' said Sender. 'Thank you for—'

'Yes, yes,' said the demon. 'Our time on this plane, Sender, is limited. Let's get straight to tachlis. You have something I need.'

'Whatever I have is yours, my lord.'

'Remorse. Do you think I could have that?'

'I'm not sure I understand.'

'It's like this, Sender. Do you know what my *tafkid* is?'

'You purpose in Creation? It's to ... it's to ... you, you're a manifestation of the Evil Inclination ... your purpose is, er ...'

'Sender, I am a Son of Lilith and we, the Sons of Lilith, are the Tutors of Souls.

'Our work is complex and difficult. And grotesquely misunderstood by the Sons of Adam. They loathe and abhor us, fear and disdain us. But it is us they should honour. Us they should praise and credit. Because without us their free will would remain untested—a stallion that never left the barn a day in his life.

'Nu, now is it our fault that the Sons of Adam are so easily misdirected by nonsense and stupidity, by selfishness, immorality and, yes, evil? Is it a demon's fault that a refined soul is as susceptible to refined temptation as a course soul is to schmutz? Is it our fault that humanity prefers wickedness and illusion to righteousness and holiness?

'Well, just between you and me, I'm beginning to think that maybe it is. Maybe we, the Sons of Lilith, are more blameworthy than we like to think. Maybe we've misunderstood our *tafkid*. Maybe we aren't here to school the Sons of Adam; maybe we're here to learn from them ... from their passion.

'You see, we demons are an equanimous lot. We do what the *Ribono Shel Olam* tasked us to do and if a soul prefers Gehenna to Heaven, well, since we lack remorse—or, rather, I should say we lack *passionate* remorse—it's all the same to us. And you Sender ... your remorse burns brighter than most. It drives you to extraordinary measures. And it's your remorse that will drive me to extraordinary measures.

'Sender, I offer you this: I will take from you the anguish of remorse and in exchange I will return your wife to the waking world. What do you say?'

Sender's answer was immediate and emphatic: 'No.'

The demon was flabbergasted. 'Think about your wife, Sender.'

'I am. That's why my answer will always be no. I beg you, make me another offer. Ask for my possessions, my good name, my freedom, ask me to transgress a commandment, ask me to commit sins, atrocities, abominations, anything—but not that.'

'There is no other offer on the table. Your wife will sleep until she dies. Unless you relinquish your remorse to me.'

Sender would not be swayed.

'Let her sleep then,' hissed the demon, nettled.

And he turned his back on Sender and Sender found himself alone in an icy field far from home.

Pearl slept. Sender prayed and he gave to charity and he made repentance. But that did no good. He even confessed to his sleeping wife. Told her of his failings. Told her of Jonas and Lukas and his dread of the scandal they would stir. Told her of Abba and of Menachem. Told her of his encounter with the demon. Spared neither detail nor himself. But that did no good either. She slept and slept and died one night in her sleep.

He waited until after her stone setting ceremony before he called on the Angel of Death. He was lying in his nightclothes in the bed in which his wife had slumbered for so many years. 'Listen,' he said, 'I know you're coming, but would it kill you to hurry?'

And such was the intensity of his *kavona*—a miracle! The Angel of Death appeared to him as a bewildering agglomeration of eyes bearing a sword tipped in poison.

But the angel would not take his life. He pointed out that on the Day of Atonement it was sealed how many shall pass away and how many will be born, who shall live and who shall die, who shall reach the end of his days and who shall not.

'That's wonderful,' said Sender, 'but right now—my children and my grandchildren never see me and without Pearl I have nothing in this world. So my remaining days? Give them to someone else. Someone who might actually do a little good in this world. Don't tell me it hasn't been done before.'

'Oy, don't remind me,' said the Angel of Death.

'Nu?'

The Angel of Death's bewildering agglomeration of eyes softened, and he said: 'I'll shuffle some paperwork and you can have your death. Naturally you get some say in who gets your remaining years. I'll narrow down the likely candidates for you. There's—'

'I don't care. Give them to anyone. Give them to someone useful, a gabbai, a washerwoman, a seamstress. Give them to the Tsar or Pobedonostsev, for all I care. I'm happy to leave the decision with you. I'm sure you have a worthy candidate in mind. Now can we please get on with it.'

'There's no point rushing a premature death. The unforeseen consequences from the slightest misstep ... well, you wouldn't believe how they reverberate from generation unto generation.'

'Fine, fine.'

'I tell you what, why don't I light you a final cigar and we can schmooze a little while we wait for the pieces to fall into place. If I might, there's something ... a little personal, perhaps, I'd like to ask you. That is, if you don't mind ...'

'Go ahead. I can't promise to answer—but you can certainly ask.'

The Angel of Death produced a cigar, lit it for Sender, and said: 'Why did you refuse his offer?'

'In all honesty,' said Sender drawing on the cigar, 'probably fear.'

'If you were so afraid of the demon, why did you summon him in the first place?'

'Oh, I wasn't afraid of the demon. And I never doubted his sincerity. I do believe he hoped to do some good with my remorse.'

'Well, then what were you afraid of?'

'Myself. I was afraid of myself. I thought of what my concern with propriety, my cravenness, my stupidity had cost Jonas and Pearl ... and that was when I was capable of remorse! Without remorse ... God knows what I might do—for whatever *meshuggener* reason!'

'And you've never regretted your decision?'

'Regretted it? I regretted it every time I stepped into Pearl's bedroom, every time I looked at her lying there so still and lifeless, every minute, every hour, every second of the day. But do you know what I never had regarding it, not for a moment?'

'No.'

'Remorse.'

Sender smiled an impish smile and the Angel of Death chuckled.

The pair fell into a contemplative and companiable silence and after a while the Angel of Death said, 'It won't be long now.'

But Sender did not hear him. He had fallen asleep, letting his lit cigar fall on his cotton bedspread where it began to smoulder and then to blaze.

Sean Shapiro was born in Belgium, spent his formative years in South Africa, and now lives in Borehamwood, England. The story which you have (hopefully) just read was inspired by his love of classic supernatural fiction and his abiding interest in Yiddish folklore and Yiddish writers of imaginative fiction like Der Nister, IL Peretz, S. Ansky and Isaac Bashevis Singer.

MEASURING MY CHILDHOOD

Mariel Herbert

Mother called it a birth defect
my right hand parted down the middle
Biblical like the sea. Her daily blessings
for the righteous did not rescue me
from children with salted fingers.

Hid my cloven hoof in the sacred
fringe of my shawl, wove prayers
in rushes and reeds. But my burning
mind overflowed chapped lips
scraped against the desks abandoned
at the front of the class. Teacher brushed
off my questions, gathered her pupils
in a parsley leaf skirt.

Taunts trailed as fins from the school bus
stuffed fish jaw, flesh flapping. I ran
through clouds of Granny Smith gas. Raw
pink skin itched, knees popped, legs locked
into salmon scales. When Mother slept
I scratched trenches, shaped ichthyic
topography beneath my mattress.

Puberty came blazing in broad daylight
raining buy-one-get-one-free gift cards

for coarse hair. Mother caught me sobbing
in the bathroom, sticking bits of toilet paper
on little piggy bristles.

She used maternal coercion, brought me
to experts to say I must fit in with girls
my age. Cattle prods buried in tsks and
spit prepared and force fed. I'm half
fish/half goat, seasoned-plated-garnished
for two Leviathan on a five-star beach--
making out all over a new world.

*Mariel writes speculative and short form poems, including haiku
and senryu. She likes to meld the mythic with the absurd. Mariel
used to live in the fog by the Pacific Ocean. Now she lives with
several mosquitos. Her poetry has been published in many lovely
places, including this year's Dwarf Stars anthology. You can find
her online at marielherbert.wordpress.com.*

THE WEDDING FEAST

Buck Weiss

The Wolf and the Thief in the Night were seated next to each other at the wedding reception of their daughters.

"It is a bit of a funny story," said the Thief in the Night. His voice had an old-world charm that made the dark-skinned lady, across the table from the fathers, tingle. She was a lovely woman who had been a House Mother to the Wolf's daughter during her MFA. She had known both girls during their courtship and was familiar with the story, but she was too polite to interrupt. "They actually met in a therapy group for children who were estranged from their parents. It's so dull, it's almost cliché."

"Well," said the Wolf, who paused for a moment to sip from his Bordeaux. "I understand my Lyall's need for a womanly influence in her life. After all, I ate her mother in front of her when she was seven."

The House Mother, who wore a lime green dress with white polka-dots and a broad brimmed hat, placed her fan over her face to hide her audible gasp.

"Wolf!" the Thief in the Night chided. "There is no need to scare the poor woman."

The Wolf scoffed. "My apologies, dear lady. No matter how we fight it or hide behind our civilized..." He looked around the beautifully decorated room. "...facades. We can only be our nature."

"The story of my entrance into fatherhood is sadly not much more jocund." The Thief in the Night gazed into the dark red of his glass of Amontillado. "I was collecting the souls of her family. There had been a gas leak and the couple had peacefully slipped away in their sleep. I gathered them into my carriage and moved quietly upstairs to her nursery. As I leaned over her crib, she lifted her little hands toward me." He paused for a moment to brush the salt of the memory from his eyes. "She caught her reflection in the blade of my sickle and cooed softly. I fell in love at first sight."

"They are all so beautiful at that age," said the House Mother.

The Thief in the Night tipped his glass.

"Tasty," said the Wolf.

"She was a teenager when I told her the story. I thought she would be happy that I had saved her from the fate of her family. It was, to use a parlance of my profession, the nail in the coffin of our happy home."

The House Mother started to speak and thought better of it.

The Thief in the Night drank deep. "Womanly influence? My dear Wolf, do not tell me you are prejudiced against the union of our only daughters?"

"Not at all," the Wolf said. "I am glad they have found each other."

"Love is love." The Thief in the Night winked at the House Mother.

Drawing up her courage, she lifted her glass of chardonnay in a toast. "To love," she said.

"To love," repeated the others with glasses lifted to each other and to lips.

"I am actually elated at the union," spoke the Wolf. "These are not times to bear young, and we do not have to worry about that here."

The Thief in the Night cringed as he sat down his glass. "You are illiberal, you old dog. How can you be unhappy about this union? Your master honored love in all its forms. His shield maidens dine alongside the men and love who they please."

"Quite the opposite of your God, Child Killer," the Wolf replied. He kept his voice low, but it was filled with more than a little venom. "He subjugates the female and persecutes those who, as you say, love who they please."

"His followers," the Thief in the Night replied. "Do not confuse the god with the blind men who misinterpret his words."

"If I may," The House Mother had gained her courage. The Thief in the Night thought she was now in the element that her boarding house provided: breaking up the fights of children.

Both stopped to look at her.

"What do you mean, 'these are not times for children'?"

The Thief in the Night waved his glass to take in the room and gave a little laugh. "He was being facetious, speaking of the end of the world."

"You can mock me all you want," said the Wolf. "But we are both waiting on the call. The clash of swords and the roar of armies. As you know. You will take the faithful to your master. I will consume what is left."

"Yet, no man will know the day or hour."

"I know the prophecies. Look around you. How can we not be in the final days?"

The Thief in the Night started to look a little nervous. "Times have been bad before. You are just ready for the end."

"Well," the Wolf replied, "your work keeps you busy. All I have is Ragnarök. I am hungry for the taste of the sun."

"Is there no joy in life?" the House Mother said. "Can you not pause to celebrate the union of your daughters."

"You are wise beyond your young years, my dear," said the Thief in the Night.

"I apologize for my morose thoughts." The Wolf extended his glass in salute.

Suddenly a trumpet sounded from the other side of the banquet hall.

The Thief in the Night jumped up, pulling his sickle from inside his robe. "I must go!" He cried.

"May I have your attention! Please rise to welcome the brides!" cried one of the best men.

A slow concerto started as everyone joined the Thief in the Night in standing. As one they all turned to the far side of the room. Double doors opened and the brides stepped through, resplendent in their matching white wedding gowns and bouquets of lilacs and lilies.

The two were caught in the dazzle of their perfect day and their perfect love. Their eyes locked on each other as the room exploded into claps and applause around them.

It was not until the couple climbed the small steps that led to the head table that they both turned towards everyone standing below them. They blew kisses to the crowd and giggled as people waved and cheered to catch the eye of each.

The Thief in the Night waited patiently for his daughter's gaze, his Eden's beautiful violet eyes. They finally fell on him, and a single tear flowed for the pride he felt in the magic of this moment.

"Sorry for the..." she mouthed from across the room. Placing a thumb to her lips, she held her hands out as if she was blowing a horn. "I didn't mean to scare you." She smiled innocently at him.

"Yes, she did!" mouthed her wife, pushing herself in front of Eden to take his line of sight. Both women laughed and fell into snuggling. They sat, their attention drawn back to the crowd of friends and loved ones before them.

The Wolf turned toward the Thief in the Night and pulled a handkerchief from his pocket to dab at his own eyes. "Your pup is a wild one. She will end up getting my innocent Lyall in all sorts of trouble."

"As I recall from their courtship," said the House Mother. "It was Lyall who had the best schemes of the two. Running naked through the quad, entering butter statues of their privates into the library's annual edible art contest and taking bets on which would win."

Both heads turned toward the House Mother and her smile melted their hearts even more. "Oh," she said. "The stories I have for you."

The Wolf and the Thief in the Night reveled in her tales of their daughter's young love as they all ate their wedding feast of chicken with caramelized onions and green beans. The plates were taken away and replaced with a fresh set for the cake when the Wolf finally laughed at the presumption of his friend. "You should have seen yourself jump when that trumpet sounded. You were ready to reap the world."

The House Mother joined in with a smile.

"I will admit," said the Thief in the Night, "that my first instinct was to duty. However, I would be remiss if I were not here to give her my gift. "

"Oh," said The Wolf. "Now, we are intrigued. The registry was long but mundane overall. I bought them a knife set."

"I was happy to see that the same brand of cappuccino machine we have at the boarding house was on the list," said the House Mother. "Gifts with intention are always best."

They both looked to the Thief in the Night expectantly.

"Well, my precious lady," he said, giving the wine in his glass a little twirl. "I am so glad you feel that way because my gift is nothing but intentional. I hope it repairs the problems Eden and I have had these past years." He took a long drink to prolong the suspense.

"I saw you place a card on the table, but no gift," she said, trying in vain to move him along.

The Wolf gave a low growl of annoyance. "Oh, dear boy. You are always the drama king. Out with it."

"As you know," the Thief in the Night continued, "My relationship with Eden has never been the same since I told her of my part in the passing of her poor parents. She has warmed up to me in the past few years, but I still feel the strain. So, I decided to salve that wound for her as my ultimate gift on the day of her wedding."

The House Mother's face turned ashen.

The Wolf shook his head, trying to dispel worried thoughts like ill omens. He turned to his friend in earnest dread. "What have you done?"

The Thief in the Night smiled. "I have brought her parents back to her."

The laughs and music of the party slipped away as the two others at the table sat there, completely foxed.

He laughed nervously as he took in their thrown faces. "Eden's parents are waiting outside in the garden. I hope to steal her away for a moment and introduce them to her once more."

The Wolf shook his great head, and the House Mother rubbed her eyes.

"What?" the Thief asked. "Isn't it brilliant?"

"I am sorry, sir," she said, sitting up to gather her courage. "I do not agree that your gift is a good one."

"What?" said the Thief in the Night. "Why?"

"Why," said the Wolf. "Only the arrogant prick who killed all the firstborn sons in Egypt would think that reuniting his daughter with the family that he took from her, and on her wedding day no less, was a good idea."

"Your barbs are getting onerous, Son of Loki!" said the Thief in the Night, more than a little offended.

The House Mother raised her hand to stop them once more. "Mr. Wolf is rough with his words, but his point is solid and it is the strong concern of a friend. Can't you see what your Eden will think of you?"

The Thief in the Night raised a shaking hand to his chest.

"If you brought them back today," she continued, "Why did you not bring them back when she was thirteen? Or when she was still a baby? In that case, why even take them in the first place?"

Tears formed in the Thief in the Night's eyes.

"I can see that you are starting to put it all together," she continued. "Poor Eden has been through therapy and support groups. She has worked hard and forgiven you. Your place here at the wedding is a big step in that reconciliation. What is she going to think when you present her with people that she never knew? People that you took away and never told her you could bring back?"

The Wolf reached over and placed a paw on his shoulder. "You are her father, my friend. We are her family now. She has no need for others."

The Thief in the Night wiped his eyes with his napkin. "What am I going to do? I have two people sitting in the garden waiting to be reunited with their daughter and I have no gift at my own daughter's wedding. I've ruined everything."

They sat there in silence for a long moment and then the House Mother raised a finger. "We can help you with this," she said. "My dear, Mr. Wolf. Was the chicken dish enough for you this evening?"

"As a matter of fact," he said, "It was barely an hors d'oeuvre. I am starving." The wolf bared his teeth and ran his long tongue over each razor-sharp barb. "Are you saying what I think you are saying?"

The House Mother nodded her head.

The Wolf leaned forward, "You, my dear are a force to be reckoned with. You have a will and reasoning that could make a demi-god blush."

"I have been the House Mother of young girls for many years. I have met more than one parent that I thought would be better for their daughter, dead." She turned toward the Thief in the Night. "If you will accept it, good sir, I will take my card from the cappuccino machine and replace it with yours. That will give you a gift."

The Thief in the Night stood and walked around the table to where his savior sat. "You, my sweet lady," he said, "Will live a long and happy life. Thank you!"

After the cake was cut and everyone had their pieces, the Wolf stood. "I believe a walk in the garden will be a welcome venture after such a small dinner."

He was back in time for toasts and, as he stood before the crowd on his hindlegs, the long brown tail sticking out the back of his three-piece suit, he bragged about the accomplishments of his amazing daughter and picked his large canine teeth with a bright white bone.

As the Thief in the Night spoke of walks in the park and teaching his Eden how to ride a bike, he saw the House Mother slide over to the gift table and slyly exchange the cards. He thanked the crowd for loving his daughter so much and thanked his lord for new friends and old.

Finally, the reception moved on to music and more merriment. The Wolf and the Thief in the Night joined their daughters for a dance. The Thief in the Night held his Eden close and tried his best to capture one more moment with her alone.

"Thank you," she said as she swayed with him and nestled into his cloak. "Thank you for coming. Thank you for everything."

"I bought you a cappuccino maker!" he blurted out.

His daughter smiled. "Really?" She paused their dance and looked intently into his shrouded face. "Wow! That is the most thoughtful gift you have ever given me. I know we are going to love it!" She pulled him close. "I love you!"

He held his daughter tightly as they danced. Somewhere off in the distance, a joyful trumpet started to play once again. The Thief in the Night tensed to fly, but his daughter clung to him as if she never wanted to let him go.

"Please, Lord," he thought. "Not today. I want to be right here forever."

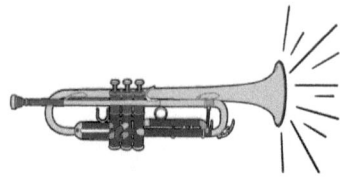

Buck Weiss (he/him) is a writer who lives in Chattanooga, TN. To read other short stories and follow his work, subscribe @buckw.substack.com.

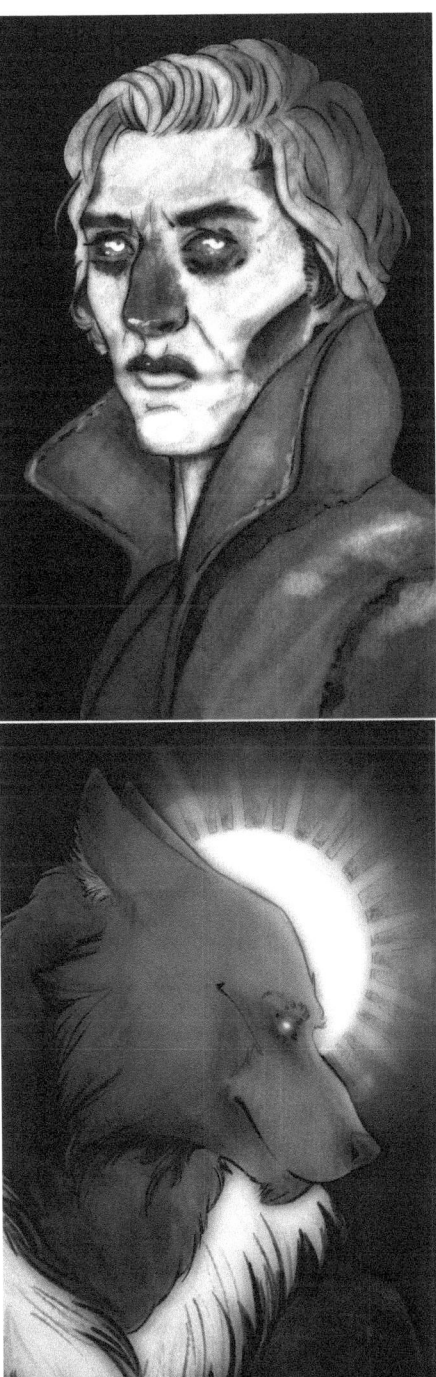

THE OARFISH BRIDE

Amelia Gorman

The oarfish is coming to conquer the beach,
the first signs are already here: the unraveling
of every banner, each emerald flag on the sea wall.

I, too, come undone. I knew the mosaics by heart.
The poems and legends were always at my fingertips,
like the wide striped ribbon around my neck.

The sea froths red with protein and slime.
Crinkled wood washes up on shore, the remains
of so many fishing boats, so many of our fishers.

My neighbor, out collecting cockles, lashed,
pulled out to sea. Her hair churns loose in the wind,
then the water. Cracks form in the sand.

Deep furrows that bubble with salt and tar,
shimmering in a hundred colors, filled with stars.
And the stars, too, come closer to kiss the lighthouse.

The oarfish is coming, I saw from the headlands
as he took a frenzy of sharks in his mouth, as he
surrounded a dinghy and squeezed the blood out of
  it.

Meanwhile I wove ribbons, also red and blue,
but green besides for the city. Silk ribbons, paper
  ribbons,
I curled and bowed and quilled until I bled.

I weave them through my hair, or what's left of it.
I wrap my legs, I tie my corset tight and gasp
like a drowning man, like a fish on the shore.

I lace my boots with indigo, I fill them with sand -
sand that is a thousand glittering mussel shells
and glass from the city midden. I fill my pockets with
  gems.

Let me be the oarfish bride, let me quell the seas,
let me untie the knots that hold us in place. Let me
  sink,
full of ribbons, on my wedding night.

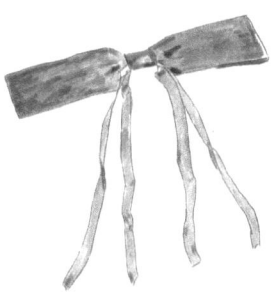

Amelia Gorman lives in Eureka where she spends her free time exploring tidepools and redwoods with her dogs and foster dogs. Her fiction has appeared in Nightscript 6 *and* Cellar Door *from Dark Peninsula Press. You can read some of her poetry in* Vastarien, Utopia Science Fiction, *and* Strange Horizons. *Her first chapbook, the Elgin-winning* Field Guide to Invasive Species of Minnesota, *is available from Interstellar Flight Press.*

TREE, GALL, SONG

Wren Douglas

Making the ink for the prophet's scriptures is an easy task. First you pick the peaches from the tree that shades the walls of the inner garden; the gods themselves planted the seed that germinated it, nursing it to health with twelve days of rains followed by twelve days of sun, and commanded a monastery to be built around it once the first sprout broke the soil.

It's the pride of the church, the tree, and the fruit in your wicker basket its most prized possession. Every week, lords and ladies come to offer you a dowry's worth of riches in the hope you'll take their daughters as apprentices, so persistent in their pursuit of divine favor you're running out of ways to say no.

A marquis recently threatened to gift you a harpsichord with real ivory keys and enough gold leaf to double its weight. The memory makes song itch under your tongue, but you squish it between your cheek and your teeth. You have to choose the right peaches, as the procedure demands. Also, the prophet's gaze is tracking you.

He approaches with placidity in the curve of his mouth, his figure cutting a narrow white line through the grass and the tuff walls; the light dances in green swaths across his face as it passes through the leaves.

No member of the church is allowed to stand in the shadow of the tree, except for you.

"My dear," he says, stretching the sound wide. His eyes lower from your face to the neckline of your robe, which folds outward as you bend to paw at a peach. "Must you always do the tedious work yourself? The sun will bake your skin at this time of the day."

You adjust your grip and pull, balancing yourself on a low branch as the bark rubs against the soles of your feet. The peach comes off its stalk with ease, warm and golden in your hand: it'll do.

"None of the children are of age to help yet," you say, careful to turn around so your hair won't get caught or your eye poked. The last peach you need is higher up, but you can reach it fine with a bit of maneuvering.

The prophet scoffs. "Of age? The oldest girl is twelve," he says. "Surely that's enough."

You shift your weight to your knee and pull yourself up onto the branch, ignoring the spike of vertigo as you snatch the last peach you need. Again, it comes off smoothly. The tree rustles around you in recognition. "Not for holy things," you say.

Oil-slick artifice coats his lips, the sign he's caught your meaning but intends to ignore it. When you swing your legs down, he catches your waist before you can make the leap and presses your bodies together, slowly lowering you to the ground; by the grace of the gods, your skirt doesn't bunch up past your mid-thigh. "Why the hurry?" he asks in your ear.

"The inkwells are empty," you say, though you don't mention you've been draining them down the privy each night, careful not to skim off too much. "They need replenishment."

A sigh that tastes of sweetened wine ghosts over the line of your neck. "Married to her duties, my priestess," the prophet says, but he puts space between the two of you at last. He makes an effort to look the pious part when he's in the open. "You'll come later, then?"

You bow your head in deference. "Of course."

———————•◦•———————

After setting the basket of peaches aside on the kitchen count-
er, you go to the fireplace and gather the charcoal in a sack,
scraping the rake against the blackened bricks. The sound com-
forts you, after the prophet's honeyed words.

You heap the charcoal into a mortar, grateful for your
gloves, and glance at the pan waiting on the stove. Usually,
you'd slice the peaches open, crush their pits and toss the innards in the pan to cook the amygdalin away. The prophet used
to make sure you'd do that every single time, back when you'd
only just succeeded the previous priestess.

Years of making perfectly safe ink for him have eased his
fears away, though, so he's not here to watch as you skip the
pan and add the softer bits directly to the charcoal, followed by
water and gum. You grind the pestle until everything is even
and well-meshed, indistinguishable from the usual. Your heart
only trembles slightly.

After you've taken your gloves off, you pop a slice of peach
into your mouth: it tastes like nectar, glazing your palate in
sunlight, and you resolve to share the rest with the children
before you go deliver the prophet his new batch of ink.

———————•◦•———————

When you succeeded the previous priestess, she explained to
you the full scope of your role. You're the tender of the tree,
tasked to nurse it like the gods and mesh its blessing with the
prophet's ink so that he may always write the truth, but you're
also the tender of the monastery. You take in children who
have nowhere else to go and you make sure the granary is full;
you handle payrolls and keep an eye out, at all times.

"One day," the old priestess said to you the day she divested
her robe, "something will grow bent out of shape, like an oak
gall full of grubs."

You still remember her unmoving stare when she said the next words, the chill in it forever fizzling where it meets your warmer memories.

"It shall fall upon you to excise it, lest it fester in our home. This, too, is your duty, as it was once mine."

The prophet's at his desk, his quill scratching the parchment in a familiar pattern of starts and stops. Earlier he greeted you by grabbing your chin and pressing a wet kiss to the corner of your mouth, emboldened by the privacy of his quarters. This is the second time he's done that, and it won't be the last.

So you watch him write. It's a long hymn he's composing, stanza after stanza of future floods, landslides, bouts of hail so violent the farmers will have to swaddle their crops in thick, waxed cloth. It used to surprise you, how mundane his scriptures were.

He's a messy writer too. His hands are painted black, ink seeping through the skin and into his bloodstream, and he licks his index finger each time he has to turn the page. His tongue flicks over the pad, comes up stained. You wish the previous priestess had told you how long it'll take for his body to convert the amygdalin into cyanide, because the wait is crawling over your bare arms like ants.

"You shan't rely on anyone's help," the old woman's voice whispers in your ear. "Given an inch, they would argue you're blowing things out of proportion. They would call you hasty, hysterical. Frigid. So you shall act alone, and dispose of their useless concerns."

You're so busy steadying your breaths you almost miss the signs. The prophet hunches over the desk, a hand pressed to his forehead, smearing ink all over the sweat-slick skin. His other hand goes to his stomach and he looks at you, addled like one of the kids when they wake up from a nightmare.

"My dear," he says, "would you fetch me a glass of water? The pitcher's on the sideboard."

"Of course," you say. Your feet carry you across the room as if they're the only thing keeping your head from floating off your shoulders to bump into the ceiling. Your hands shake when they close around the pitcher, but the condensation is blessedly cool against your palms.

You focus on the shape of the droplets while the prophet vomits, moaning syllables that could slur together into your name. If the poison isn't enough to kill him, you'll have to finish the job yourself. Excise the gall and crush the grubs under your heel.

The prophet once showed you where he keeps his knife—an exquisite mother-of-pearl blade he was gifted by a heiress, likely in the hopes he would write of her land in his hymns or put in a good word with you. You unglue your hands from the pitcher, wiping them on your robe, and turn to the desk, ready to rifle through its drawers with a poisoned man writhing on the floor next to you. Your nerves are not so frayed you wouldn't kick him in the head if he grabbed for your legs.

When you look down, though, he's crawling to the door. There is a frenzied light in his eyes, his mouth dribbling with bile as he cries for help.

Panic streaks through you. How would you explain this, if he got a hold of someone? If he got a hold of the antidote he demands you're always fully stocked with, and then branded you a crazed heretic? Your lungs gasp for air, as if submerged. You need to get that knife before he gets to the door, but your body is rooted in place, cursing the prophet for his lechery and the former priestess for her burden and most of all yourself, for this gutless display in the face of your duty.

Your skin is cold and you can't breathe through the stink of puke.

Then, children's laughter fills the room. They must be racing down the hallway, calling for each other like a flock of birds as they rush to the mess hall for dinner. Their chittering drowns out the prophet's pleas with talk of cakes and roasted yam.

He sucks in a stuttering inhale, but blood sprays out instead of words. One hand claws at the wood of the door, pale as bone and just as rigid; it falls with a wet slap when the prophet slumps forward, face-down in his own sickness.

A second passes in which you can only stare, obsessively checking for any movement in his chest. Then time starts again and you lurch forward, lunging for the curtained window; when you yank it open, the sight of the tree greets you, unchanged by your act. Its branches stand solid and its leaves strive upward, their edges tinged gold by the light.

Your lungs fill again. You don't spare the body a second glance as you climb onto the windowsill, nor as you leap down into the grass. No hands grab fistfuls of your flesh, and your skirt sways gently at your ankles.

When you put your hands to the bark, the tree sighs.

It was just a gall, it murmurs in its wind-chime language of rustles and creaks. The shade of the canopy cools the nervous heat on your skin, slows your squallish heart. *I've endured many and many more I will endure.*

You close your eyes as the sweetness washes over you, breathing in the peaches and resin and soil. Chasing away the taste of sickness. When song itches under your tongue again, you let it go.

Wren Douglas is an SFF author based in Italy, where they live with their devilish cats and one sprightly old dog. Their work has been featured in the 2023 Lambda finalist anthology XENO-CULTIVARS: Stories of Queer Growth, *among other venues. When they're not writing, they like to spend their free time going on walks, napping with their cats and playing tabletop RPGs.*

DEMETER'S LAMENTATION

Elena S. Kotsile

Under acidic sky I was
stood upon sterile rock
staring single strands
swimming unsheathed
in elemental oceans.

Now, only death.
Death of the deer.
Death of the tree.
Death of the wheat.

My womb weeps beneath
Hera's milk, the starry
swathe that in times past
brightened your path.

Now only darkness.
Disease, famine, and thirst
flood your world—you, who
so cruelly dismissed my
fruit and dissipated my own.

My breasts bleed your bound extinction.
My tears helpless against your fires.

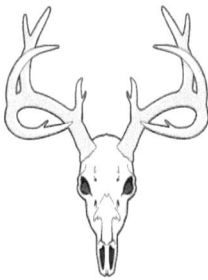

Elena S. Kotsile (pen name) is a science editor and a neurodivergent writer based in Berlin, Germany. Her creative words have appeared in various venues, such as The Future Fire, Stadtsprachen Magazin, Acropolis Journal, Grim & Gilded, Air & Nothingness Press, *and Greek journals and anthologies. Besides scientific articles, she writes speculative poetry and fiction in English and Greek. Nominated for the Rhysling Award and Best of Net. Twitter: Elena Kotsile @ElenaKotsile; Instagram: @elena_kotsile*

TO SOOTHE THE SPIRIT

Valerie Hunter

Lan came across the field of wildflowers suddenly on one of the evening walks that he felt compelled to take even when he was exhausted from a long day plowing. Somehow keeping his feet moving kept his mind from completely racing away, going places he didn't want it to dwell.

But when he came across that field just beyond his own property, everything stopped. He stood still, and the only thought in his head was the absolute beauty of it. He drank it in— the array of colors and shapes, the earthy scent, and the movement of the flowers' dance in the slight breeze. He'd been numb for so long that it was a shock to realize he could still feel such awe and wonder deep in his bones.

He stayed until the sun set. He had to stumble home in the dark, and all but fell into bed, sleeping so deeply that his nightmares didn't wake him like they usually did. Perhaps he managed to avoid them altogether; he couldn't remember when he woke up.

He returned to the flowers the next evening, and every evening after that. The sight wasn't the same glorious shock that it had been that first time, but it was still wondrous, still managed to soothe something inside of him every time. He came to appreciate the individual flowers, none of which he knew the names of— the yellow ones with their wild, asymmetrical petals; the blues so deep he could almost drown in them; the delicate purple ones that were rarest and most beautiful. Did flowers like this exist all over the countryside, or was this some kind of magic?

He rubbed at his arm. No, magic would never be used for something so frivolous. Besides, no mages had come to the new territory. It was part of its appeal to Lan, who had claimed a homestead in the area nicknamed the Back End of Nowhere because he couldn't think of anywhere else to go. Certainly not home; he didn't have the nerve for that. He loved his family, but they seemed to belong to a different Lan, that pre-war boy that he had trouble believing was him. If he'd gone back to them, they'd want him to still be that boy, and that would break him. Or else they'd accept him for who he was now, and that might break something in *them*. He didn't want to be responsible for that.

So he wrote them bland letters that bordered on cheerfulness because he could almost manage to be his old self for the duration of a letter. He pretended he was enjoying his independence, enjoying farming, when in truth he was just surviving.

He'd tried his best. Built himself a soddie and told himself that he didn't mind living in such a small, suffocating abode made out of the earth himself. He was little better than an animal, but wood was dear out here and he needed shelter. He focused on surviving, plowing as many acres as he could manage with his sorry mules and his sorry self. He still looked as though he might snap in half in a strong wind, but if he took it slow, he could manage.

He liked being outdoors, breathing in the clean air and not being able to see another soul. The neighbors were far enough away that he rarely saw them— a broad-shouldered, one-armed man named Uster on one side, and a woman, Demyra, on the other. Neither seemed inclined to socialize, which suited Lan just fine. He didn't need anyone.

The Back End of Nowhere was the antithesis of the prison camp in Corett. Even the sky and the sun overhead seemed different. He tried to convince himself he was in a completely different world, but he only truly believed that when he was looking at those wildflowers.

It was, perhaps, a little like an addiction. He didn't realize how much he depended on seeing the flowers until it rained one evening. He contemplated going anyway, but after seeing a flash of lightning, he thought better of it. Of course he should stay in.

And so he did, but he slept poorly. He told himself it was the walk he missed, that last bit of physical exertion that made him sleep soundly, but he knew it was really the flowers. When morning came, the sun bright and the sky cloudless, he set out across the fields as though he might perish if he had to wait until evening to see them again.

They were still damp from last night's rain, and seemed to shimmer ever so slightly in the newly risen sun. He wondered how the same sun could rise here as rose in Corett, how such extremes of beauty and ugliness could exist in the world, how he could set eyes on both of them. Was anyone else from the prison camp looking at such beauty now? Was—

"It's the most glorious spot in the whole countryside, isn't it?" a voice behind him asked, and Lan flinched. He turned as she added, "Sorry. Didn't mean to startle you."

It was the woman from the neighboring claim, Demyra, along with her thin brown dog, who pushed its wet nose into Lan's fingers. He tried to collect himself. "It is glorious," he said, attempting a smile that felt wrong on his lips. He was too out of practice.

"Anyhow, I'll let you get on with your morning," she said, and was walking away before he could think of a response, the dog gamboling at her feet.

———◦◦———

After that Lan went for a walk each morning as well as the evening. He told himself he was building up stamina, but really he just needed to drink in those flowers like a tonic, fill his head with their rich colors and his nose with the balm of their scent twice a day to keep himself going.

He frequently saw Demyra in the mornings. They exchanged hellos and not much else, but he found himself looking forward to that, too. He didn't need anyone, but it was still nice to be acknowledged, to know he wasn't the last person on earth. He judged her to be around his age, perhaps a little older since a person was supposed to be twenty-one to claim land in the new territory. (Veterans were exempt from this rule; if you were old enough to have fought, no one questioned whether you were old enough to farm.)

He didn't ask her why she'd decided to come out here, as that was none of his business. She seemed more than capable; she was near as tall as Lan and sturdier, and she'd managed to break more acreage than him with the help of her hired boy, a coltish youth who didn't look more than thirteen.

Occasionally they'd discuss how the crops were doing, or what tasks they had planned for the day. When he mentioned he needed to sure up the roof of his soddie, she offered him the assistance of Guz, her hired boy, and though Lan was on the verge of refusing, he found himself saying yes instead. Truth be told, he wasn't sure how he could manage without a second set of hands.

The next day Demyra sent Guz over as promised, and they got to work. Guz was diligent, doing his best to make up for lack of size with sheer determination. Between the two of them they managed in two days what most men could have probably done in one, but Lan told himself it wasn't a race, and he appreciated the help even if he wished he didn't need it.

At the end of the second day, he gave Guz a coin and told him to come to supper tomorrow and to bring Demyra with him.

"And Caraway?" Guz asked.

It took Lan a moment to realize Caraway was the dog, but then he nodded. "And Caraway."

By the next morning he was already regretting this attempt at neighborliness. He couldn't remember the last time he'd eaten a proper meal with other people, and the thought of small talk with Demyra in the confines of the soddie rather than the edge of the field of wildflowers made him shudder. In the end he decided to move his table outside and eat in the open. He worried she'd think it was strange, but he did it anyhow because it was a comfort to have space, to be able to see the wide blue sky.

He tried his best with the meal, and had it ready to serve as Demyra, Guz, and Caraway came across the fields toward him. He ignored the twinge in his stomach and set the table.

Demyra brought a barley loaf that nearly undid him; he couldn't stomach anything with barley. It had been one of the staples at Corett, if barley littered with bugs and mixed with sawdust could be considered a staple. Of course Demyra's loaf was undoubtedly lovely and vermin-free, but he knew he couldn't eat it, and he stumbled over his thanks.

Demyra, meanwhile, complimented the meal and the idea of sitting outdoors. She talked of the weather and how well the crops were doing, and when she didn't speak the silences managed not to seem awkward.

Guz was mainly quiet, shoveling food in his mouth like he thought it might disappear if he paused overlong. Lan could remember being thirteen, when it seemed like no matter how much he ate he was still hungry. Now food never seemed to sit right in his belly, as though going for so long without had transformed his innards. He ate slowly, hoping it would make it seem as though he was eating more than he was.

Guz wasn't fooled. "You don't eat more'n a fly."

"Be polite, Guz," Demyra murmured.

"What? It's true. You'll make yourself ill that way."

Lan swallowed the lump in his throat. "I've been ill," he replied. He wasn't sure if it was a lie. Corett was hardly an illness, but it had broken his health, hadn't it? "Can't stomach too much food at once."

"That why you're such a beanpole?" Guz asked while Demyra hissed his name again.

"I reckon so."

"Well, if you need any more help around the place, you let me know."

Lan knew the boy was probably thinking of the extra money he might make rather than any altruistic motive, but he nodded anyway and said, "I will."

The meal ended pleasantly enough, and Guz helped him wrestle the table back inside. Afterwards Lan walked them to the edge of the property, then circled around to the wildflowers. Their colors seemed particularly rich tonight, and he breathed deeply and tried to float in them.

———————◆◆◆———————

The next morning he saw Demyra again. "Thank you for having us to supper," she said as though she hadn't already thanked him last night. "We'll return the favor soon."

"You needn't," he said quickly, only realizing how harsh the words sounded after they'd fallen from his mouth. "Sorry. I didn't mean..."

"It's all right." She paused. "I don't mean to be nosy, and I didn't want to ask yesterday in front of Guz because he'd badger the life out of you, but... did you fight? In the war?"

How to answer that? He kept his eyes on the deep blue of a flower, the same color as the tunic he'd worn. How had he never seen the similarity before? "I joined up when I was eighteen," he said carefully. "Two summers ago."

"I thought as much. You remind me of the soldiers I've known. It takes time to move on from such an experience, doesn't it?"

He wanted to laugh and say he didn't know. But more than anything, he didn't want to pretend to be something he wasn't. "I never even saw a battle. Got captured during a patrol, and spent the rest of the war in Corett."

"Goodness, how terrible," Demyra said, and he was surprised to hear genuine sympathy in her tone. When he dared glance at her, she added, "I heard about Corett. You were lucky to survive."

He wanted to ask what she'd heard. Surely if she knew the truth, that the prisoners had been bled, used for blood magic against their own army, she wouldn't be so sympathetic.

But he kept his mouth shut, wishing he hadn't said anything at all. He barely knew this young woman; why had he told her as much as he had?

He mumbled a quick good-bye and walked home, busying himself in farm tasks for the rest of the day. He didn't go on his evening walk even though he never saw Demyra in the evenings, nor did he go the next morning. He told himself he didn't need it, ignoring his growing twitchiness and his sleeplessness at night. Talking to Demyra had undone something within him, and all he wanted to do was button it back up.

Finally, late on the third afternoon, the antsy feeling overcame him and he headed towards the field. Only the flowers could soothe him.

When he got there he blinked, unable to comprehend what he was seeing.

Carnage. The flowers mown down like bodies, destroyed and cast aside to be replaced by neat furrows. He could see Uster walking away in the distance with his oxen, as though it was all in a day's work to destroy a bit of paradise for the sake of planting an acre of late potatoes.

Lan had never gotten into a true fight in his life, but right now his entire body shook with the urge to run after this man, pitch into him, pound him into the ground, bury him beneath the destroyed flowers. He had just enough self-control left to not actually do this, but the desire coursed through his blood until he was afraid he might burst, and then something did burst, and he was sobbing.

He didn't think he could stop. His mind was a quagmire of too many emotions that couldn't be named, but the tiny portion that could still grasp a thought was aware that never in his life had he cried like this, never in his life had he unleashed such a torrent of feelings, and therefore he had no idea how to spool them back in. He was going to empty every last thing inside of him, and once he had—once he had—

Something enveloped him, a gentle pressure on both arms, and then a voice in his ear, just loud enough that he could hear it above his own cries. "All right. It's all right."

Demyra.

He tried to tell her it wasn't. Tried to apologize for the state he was in, tried to explain, tried to ask her to leave him be. But he was incapable of forming coherent words, just continued to cry, choking back the sobs because it was terribly shameful to cry in front of another person, but he couldn't stop, couldn't—

"It's all right," she repeated, keeping a tight hold on him as though she knew how close he was to shattering. "You're all right. You'll be all right."

She kept saying it until, at long last, the tears subsided. He felt drained, dazed. Demyra's arms were still snaked around him, possibly the only thing holding him together. Caraway sat beside him, a small sentinel.

"Let's take a walk," Demyra said quietly, the way someone might talk to a spooked horse or a cringing dog. He let her lead him away because perhaps that was all he was now, just a dumb beast who went to pieces over something as simple as flowers.

"I'm sorry," he said, finally finding his voice.

"What for?"

He didn't have words enough for that.

"You've nothing to be sorry for." Her voice was still quiet, but it was fierce now, too, needle-sharp, as though it was very important he heard her. "You should never have to apologize for feelings."

They kept walking, and he realized she was leading him towards her soddie. He wanted to tell her that wasn't necessary, that he might as well go to his own soddie and attempt to pretend that none of this had happened (an impossible task, yet one he was eager to try), but his voice still didn't seem to be working properly.

Guz was in the yard feeding the chickens, and he gaped when he saw Lan, but Demyra just waved Guz away and steered Lan around the side of the soddie, where he stumbled to a halt, staring.

"Not the same, I know, but I thought you might appreciate it all the same," she said.

Flowers. Not nearly as many as in the desecrated field, but just as vibrant and riotous. More variety, more colors. He'd never seen a garden so wild. His mother's back home had been orderly and completely soulless, everything in careful rows. This was chaos, an explosion of blooms, though he could tell Demyra must have planned it carefully.

There was a little bench, and Demyra sat, pulling him down with her. Caraway plopped himself on Lan's feet, a warm anchor.

"I did so much planting for food and livelihood that I figured I owed it to myself to plant something for sheer happiness, too," Demyra said.

"Very wise," he said quietly, and then added, "I didn't even realize that field was Uster's land."

"I don't know that it is, actually. I think he figured he'd take advantage of a little stretch that didn't belong to anyone."

Lan could feel his chest hitch and shudder, and he willed himself not to cry again. What was done was done. "You must think me a terrible fool."

She frowned. "What did I say about apologizing?"

"I don't think I've ever cried like that in my life," he admitted.

"Then you were overdue. All the things you went though, as a soldier...maybe it was time to shed some tears."

He scoffed. "I wasn't much of a soldier. I never even saw a battle, remember?"

"Didn't you live through one every day you were in that prison?"

He shut his eyes, shook his head. "Not a battle, no, just...a nightmare to be endured. There wasn't enough food, or space, or...anything, really." They'd been penned up like animals, kept for one purpose. Blood couldn't come from a corpse. "Every month the blood-letting... knowing that your blood was being used for magic against your own people..."

"Both sides did it," Demyra said quietly.

"Doesn't make it right."

"No."

"Sometimes I think I haven't woken up yet. From that nightmare."

A hand closed over his, and he opened his eyes, looked over at Demyra who had a strange expression on her face. "Can I tell you something?" she asked, and her voice sounded similarly strange, even strangled.

He tried to pull himself back to the here and now. "Of course."

She nodded but remained silent another few moments, continuing to stare at the flowers as though they might provide her with the words she was looking for. "It's a war story," she said finally.

"All right." Her hand was still on top of his, and he wiggled out from under it and held it properly, as though that might help.

"We were orphaned as babies," she said. "Me and my twin brother Berdie. We only ever had each other. We got passed around to all sorts of relations and neighbors and..." Her voice caught for a moment, but she cleared her throat and went on. "But anyhow, we always managed to stay together. He was all the family I needed."

Lan had two brothers, both good men whom he loved, but he was pretty sure he had never spoken of them, or any other member of his family, with the love and reverence that was in Demyra's voice right now.

There was sadness, too. He already knew the ending to this story, didn't he? He didn't need to have it told, but he got the feeling Demyra needed to tell it, so he kept quiet.

"The war began when we were fourteen, and two years later Berdie decided he was going to go. We were living with a cousin and his wife then. They weren't...they weren't good people. They weren't family, even if they were blood. So I told Berdie if he was going, I was going with him. And I did."

She paused. Lan tried to sort out what, exactly, she was saying, and came up short.

"I joined the king's army," she said, as though realizing she'd have to say it outright in order for him to comprehend. "Pretended to be a boy."

He stared at her as though this might make her words make more sense. "And that...worked?"

She gave a short laugh. "It did. No one questioned it. We were just two brothers doing our duty. I'm sure they suspected we weren't eighteen, but they took us anyway. No one but Berdie knew I was Demyra and not Dem."

He continued to stare, trying to piece her into his memories of the war. The two refused to go together. Surely she must have been found out quickly; surely she hadn't had to live through the misery or the horror or the—

"Stop looking at me like that," Demyra said, and he turned his gaze back to the flowers instead, his mind still balking.

"Did you..." He took a deep breath and tried again. "The whole rest of the war?"

"The whole rest of the war. Two years of pretending to be someone I wasn't, until sometimes I nearly forgot who I was. Pretend long enough and it starts to feel real, eh?"

He nodded. That was what he'd done in Corett, wasn't it? Pretended to be a man instead of a boy, pretended he was brave and not terrified, pretended away one moment at a time until he'd finally been freed, only to find he couldn't get his own self back.

"It wasn't so bad as long as I had Berdie. We never talked about it, never had a moment's privacy, but knowing he knew I was Demyra felt like...oh, I don't know, an anchor of sorts.

"But he died seven months in. Got bad sick in his belly. Seems a silly thing to die of in the middle of a war. Hardly heroic."

"Death usually isn't," Lan said, thinking of all the terrible deaths he'd witnessed, men rotting away with illness and starvation, perishing from lack of hope as much as loss of blood.

"No, I suppose not. Anyhow, I thought of deserting after Berdie passed, but it hardly seemed worthwhile. I didn't have anywhere to go back to, and I felt loyal to my mates. I was a soldier, for better or worse, so I got on with being one."

"You saw battle," he said. It wasn't a question because he knew she must have, but it horrified him to envisage it.

"I did. The terrible part was right before, that feeling you'd get in the pit of your stomach like the world was about to end. In the midst of it, everything just moved quickly, there was no time to think. And after, you just wanted to forget, to feel glad you survived and joke around with your mates and try to pretend you'd never have to do it again."

Her hand was still in his, and he squeezed it because he didn't know what to say, just wanted to remind her he was here.

"Anyhow, I survived. Thought about staying Dem, but there didn't seem much point. So I came out here and became Demyra again. Tried to figure out what that meant.

"That was late last summer. I was fine for a while. I discovered the field of wildflowers, and it just about bowled me over with its beauty. But when winter came..." She shook her head. "The cold and the snow, and being stuck inside with my thoughts and my memories, all alone...there were days I thought I might go mad. Days I was sure I already had. So I made plans for the future, for my hope and my happiness. Dreamed of the garden I'd have come spring. Made arrangements to get myself a dog and a hired boy, someone else who had nobody, just like I did. Made myself a home and a family because that was what I needed."

"To forget?" he asked.

"Nah. No forgetting, is there? But it helped me move on. Create a self I could live with. I'll have always been the orphan and the soldier, but I'm someone else now, or at least I'm trying to be."

Was it really as simple as that? He let his eyes wander around the tumult of flowers. No, not simple. The garden, the homestead, the being responsible for other living things, be they boy or dog, all of that took effort, didn't it? All of that took trying. All of that took giving of yourself, taking a chance, continuing to hope.

As did telling your greatest secret to a neighbor you barely knew, just because you realized he needed to hear it.

"Thank you," he said. "For telling me all that. For sharing this with me." He gestured to the garden. "Do you know all their names?"

"Most of them. Phlox. Anemone. Mallow. Aster. Larkspur. Fritillaries. Eglantine." He followed her pointing finger, feeling as though he was being introduced to friends.

"I always wanted a garden," she said. "I never stayed in one place long enough to grow one, or had anyone willing to let me. There's something about flowers that just..." She trailed off, shaking her head.

"Soothes the spirit?" he offered.

Demyra smiled, a slow and radiant bloom. "Exactly that," she agreed, and they sat there in comfortable silence and appreciated the view.

Valerie Hunter teaches high school English and has an MFA in writing for children and young adults from Vermont College of Fine Arts. Her stories have appeared in publications including Beneath Ceaseless Skies, Capsule Stories, OFIC, *and* Sonder, *as well as multiple anthologies.*

LETTER FROM THE EDITORS

Greetings Boneyard,

Our first two issues were built from the stories and poems we received during our first submission period, so we have sat on these for months in eager anticipation for you to finally read them. It is exciting to now have them out in the world.

This issue deals heavily with the concept of grief in its many different forms. Such topics can be inherently difficult to face, so we thank you for reading. The ways that we react to traumatic experiences—from the horrors of war, those weaponizing religion against their followers, or losing someone to their own hubris—and how we continue to live past them is where our focus tends to lie. Though many of these stories may fill you with a sense of unease, look for the glimmers of hope and humanity that live within them. We hope that these stories are ones you will reflect upon, just as they have been for the three of us.

I would be remiss if I didn't carve out a portion of this letter to give our thanks to everyone who has joined us along this journey. Whether you picked up this issue out of pure curiosity or if you have been supporting us upon the release of our first issue earlier this year, it means a lot to us. We have been able to meet other publishers and writers within the Pittsburgh writing community, and to say that *Baubles From Bones* has received a wonderfully warm reception would be an understatement. As always, a huge shoutout to our friends, family, and peers. Your words of encouragement and enthusiasm towards this quirky little zine fills us with continued fervor to embolden the voices of immensely talented authors.

From our little cryptid cave to yours,
- Shane Gallaher

BAUB'S READS

*Books and stories
we want to share*

From Joel: Are you a high fantasy nerd that loves getting embroiled in politics, relationships and dense worldbuilding but get real sad when the politics get half the cast massacred? Well then, Katherine Addison's *The Goblin Emperor* is for you! It's a high fantasy, political slice-of-life with a thick appendix of names and locations that champions friendship and bridgebuilding well above political gain. It's a delight!

Elyse says: My favorite story from recent memory is *Stardust* by Neil Gaiman. Too-simply put, it's a wonderful fantasy and tasteful love story about two young people thrust into a journey they didn't expect or want. I'd recommend it to anyone feeling a little lost, or alone under the vastness of possibility.

Shane's pick: *The Poppy War* by R.F. Kuang is definitely a book that I would recommend to a well-versed fantasy lover, or someone who is looking to try a fantasy series that is reminiscent of stories they may already know. This novel derives from the classic European fantasy but takes place in a world based on historical Chinese events. It covers some heavy topics, but I feel that this is a great introductory fantasy book, or a great way to diversify your bookshelf.

THE BONEYARD

*Special thanks to the patrons
who help support* BFB

Gaggle of Ghouls

($1 per month on Patreon or cumulative support of $1-20)

Anonymous

Patricia Enger

Anna

Skelly Bellies

($5 per month on Patreon or cumulative support of over $50)

Jayda Troutman   Johnny Morris

Caroline Ritzert   Anonymous

Anonymous

Zachary Blanner

Ron McNerney

Dylan Zeh

JM Thrower

Baubles From Bones is an independently produced and funded publication. It's our passion project! While passion can carry us through late night editing sessions and hours of slush reading, it does not pay writers, cover artists, or the cost of a printing run. That's where regular support through places like Patreon and Ko-fi comes in, helping us budget each issue and maintaining what few shreds of sanity we have left.

Our supporters get credited in print and on our website, gain access to our Discord server (where you can chat with us and our authors), and receive a copy of each upcoming issue of *Baubles From Bones*.

With additional support, we hope to release audio versions of our stories and raise pay rates for our writers and artists.

If you're excited about what we're doing and want to help fund future issues of *BFB*, consider supporting us at patreon.com/baublesfrombones or ko-fi.com/baublesfrombones.

CONVENTIONS
Come say hi!

We're tabling a few conventions this fall around Western Pennsylvania and Ohio. If you're in the area, you can say hi, pick up a copy of *Baubles From Bones*, and even get some other goodies! We have stickers, bookmarks, and little zines available, the selection of which will change from con-to-con. Be sure to come by and check them out!

WPA *Cryptid and Supernatural Expo* · · · · · · · *Sept 28-29*
Lit Youngstown: Fall Literary Festival · · · · · · · *Oct 17-19*
Scribble House Lit Fest · · · · · · · · · · · · · · · · · *Nov 17*

COVER ART
Shugarkyub

Shugarkyub, also known as Sagar, is an India-based artist who likes to tell stories with lighting and color.

You can find more of Shugarkyub's amazing work at:
www.artstation.com/shugarkyub

THIS ISSUE HAS MET ITS END, *BUT THERE'S MORE ONLINE!*

Check out our website where we catalog all of our issues for online consumption. You can also learn more about how the graveyard is dug by keeping an eye on our blog posts and, if you want to see your own work in *BFB*, sign up for our writer's mailing list to get a shout whenever our submission period reopens.

Stay up to date on new releases and bear witness to our tomfoolery by following us on Instagram: @bfb.zine.

Peruse our Etsy store where you can buy physical or digital copies of the zine, stickers inspired by our stories, and other bookish goodies!

If you want to get in touch, send us a message through the contact form on our website, DM us on Instagram, or if you're a Patreon supporter, say something in the Discord! We may present as undead, but everyone at *BFB* is always down for a lively chat!

baublesfrombones.com - *@bfb.zine* - *etsy.com/baublesfrombones*

THE BAUBLES FROM BONES TEAM

Pictured left to right we have: Caroline Ritzert, social media manager and STEM woman; Elyse Leskovic, editor, artist, and saleswoman extraordinaire; Shane Gallaher, editor and local cryptid; and Joel Troutman, editor, typesetter, and resident cook.

———◆◆◆———

Baubles From Bones is a Pittsburgh-based zine made up of four human beings with full-time jobs that are not related to this publication or our college degrees. Operating from our living room, we put this zine together during late night meetings and bleary-eyed reading sessions. Funding primarily comes from our own pockets, and profits are a dream we don't dare let ourselves believe in (though they would be nice). In our precious free time, we can often be found haunting our local parks, slurping ramen, and shopping for more books than we can read.

Thank you for giving our zine a chance and reading the incredible work our authors have sent us. We hope you come back for the next one! ☺

Baubles From Bones: Issue 2
1st Edition of 50 copies
_20_ of 50